Slanderley

Love and Death in Cornwall

Clarice Stasz

Copyright © 2016 by **Clarice Stasz**
The moral right of the author has been asserted.

All rights reserved. No part of this publication may be reproduced, distributed or transmitted in any form or by any means, without prior written permission.

**D Street Press
Petaluma, CA
www.claricestasz.com**

Publisher's Note: This is a work of fiction. Names, characters, places, and incidents are a product of the author's imagination. Locales and public names are sometimes used for atmospheric purposes. Any resemblance to actual people, living or dead, or to businesses, companies, events, institutions, or locales is completely coincidental. Any resemblance to fictional characters may not be coincidental in a work of satire or parody such as this.

Book and Cover Layout © 2014 BookDesignTemplates.com
Cover Photo Source: Fotosearch
Photo Editor: Jane Skoler

Slanderley/ Clarice Stasz. -- 1st ed.
ISBN 978-0-9967693-0-3
eISBN 978-0-9967693-1-0

To Michael

"The suspense is terrible.
I hope it will last."
Oscar Wilde

A Dreadful Return

Last night I dreamt I went to Slanderley again. From a distance in silhouette it seemed a craggy tor crowning a primeval forest. Then the moon broke through a ghostly cloud, its light catching the swirling mists off the nearby sea, creating an illusion of aerial waves. The chimneys of the ancient house resembled the broken masts of a ship wrecked centuries ago. Just as the moon crept behind another haunting cloud, the unexpected darkness left me straining for signs of life. But the silence was of a tomb.

Like all dreamers, I found myself transported without sign of travel onto the terrace of the house itself. A soft glow from candlelit rooms illumined the nearby gardens. The scent of lilacs, almost deathly sweet, left me feeling faint. Leaning upon a baluster for support, I turned toward the morning room, expecting Ravina to step out, as she often did on those sultry nights when the house was empty of guests. Thinking no one was watching, she would slip off her shoes to run down the lawn barefoot to the azalea garden, where she would wash her face in blossoms and entertain them with twinkly airs from Gilbert and Sullivan.

Some evenings she would turn around laughing, turquoise silk swishing around her sinewy hips, waving a peacock feather in her hand. "I see you there, Eddie," she would call. "Come out from behind the pillar."

To which I would straighten my butler's coat and respond, "Yes, madam, may I bring you anything?"

The dream did not return her. Instead, a shattering crash startled me. I turned around, heart pounding in my throat like a Scots guard tattoo to glimpse Scraps, the kitchen cat, flee from the remains of a potted pelargonium he had pushed over. Fortunately it was not my favorite variety, "Mrs. Henry Cox."

But Scraps, dear Scraps, had long ago entered the great feline beyond and revealed his extra lives only in dreams. Ravina too was gone, too far away to serve even as a ghost in a nighttime fantasy.

The vision continued. I was next in the great hall of that baronial home, facing its double staircase and fireplace, remnants of the banquet room of the original estate built hundreds of years earlier. Large enough to enwrap several people in conversation, the hearth was ablaze with gigantic oaken logs of a size no longer found, while the room remained cold and clammy. I sneezed so hard the fire went out.

My head tossed back, I noticed the ceiling frescoes of more recent vintage, a boisterous romp of discreetly draped gods and goddesses floating in candy sugar clouds. My original impression remained, that it was a competent if uninspired attempt by some past colorist to reproduce Verio's decorations at Hampton Court.

Excited to be within Slanderley, I rushed to seek out my favorite places. In the long drawing room, where I had spent so many pleasant hours showing guests the furniture, the oldest and most treasured remnants of the estate, all under the watchful eyes of the ancestors in their life-sized portraits. The paintings were of fair quality, considering they were by local artists in this isolated coastal community so far from the cultural graces of London. I inhaled to catch a hint of the fine lemon oils used to polish the rich grains of the tables, but coughed to the harsh odor of a stale acridness, a spoiled fruit.

Into the morning room, I gasped at its silk-paneled walls, its mirrors repeating the airy reflections from the many glassed doors to the terrace. The velvet upholstery matched the pastel shades of the thick ancient Kerman carpet. About the room stood soldiered vases of rhododendrons, each arranged as if a unique work of art to further echo the hues of the furnishings. Turning about, I saw my image fractured in a broken mirror.

The writing desk was set as on any early morning for the lady of the house, with fresh paper of faintest pomegranate, engraved in the unconventional style of Ravina, an "RdeL" in the left corner and "Slanderley" in the right. Above the pigeon holes her distinctly scratchy hand had penned categories on labels held within brass inserts: Menus, Letters to Keep, Dogs, Seed Lists, Boat Maintenance, Sloth, Hue of the Day.

How could I resist opening the drawer with the wine-colored book, *Guests at Slanderley*, divided into weeks and months to record to who had come when, their assigned rooms, their foibles and preferences? It opened upon a 1934 August Bank Holiday.

Amanda Dap: *Gherkin Room.* Still the practical joker. Spooned jam into the goulashes and peppermint oil into the cream pots. Must remember to invite to the next Briar and Bramble Collector's Outing.

Max Mallobar: *Haunted Tower.* The ever dashing and handsome archeologist. But that new wife of his! Obviously older. Always poking about and mumbling about poisons and mistaken identities.

"Boy" Tillie: *Old Dungeon.* Such a divine dancer. Still, he is so annoying with his dietary fads. Told him if he wants Muggety Pie that he'll have to bring his own sheep entrails next time.

Maud Culm: *Horseradish Room.* Not bad for a nymphomaniac. Keep her away from Eddie.

Nicholas Pickleby. *Prune Room.* One of Algernon's investment friends. Face like a prune too.

Turning the pages, I envisioned each weekend, ball, or hunt, unable to hold in tears recalling those joyous hours. Despite Slanderley's isolation, Ravina enchanted guests from hundreds of miles away to swoon over her inventive entertainments and décor.

As I opened to the last completed page, gleaming rubies flowed along the fold of the book. A rivulet flowed toward my hand. Terrified, I thrust the book away, hitting a mirror, which splintered and scattered pieces to the floor in a cascade of tear-like diamonds.

Perhaps to soften this now nightmare, I found myself in the midst of my favorite room, the library, so properly masculine. Within its darkened oak panels lingered chairs custom-fitted from years of individual use. A stone-carved fireplace interrupted glass cabinets lined with a bibliophile's dream, books bound of richest leather and craftsmanship. The volumes represented the requirements for entering an Oxbridge college. Though no fire lit this room, it was warm and stuffy. A faint odor of Lucy, the deceased basset hound, permeated the air from the hearthrug where she often lay, her tail athump when she heard her master's footfall.

This sense of familiar tranquility ended with the loud hoot of an owl. A stentorian gust of wind blew through a window's open panes, sending the draperies in furious waltzes, the lamps and knickknacks on the tables jumping like loose bones. A large antlered trophy fell atop me, waking me up.

It was a familiar dream. The house a tomb, a residence of dead memories—pleasures, fears, sufferings, shocks. Why did this nighttime exhumation recur? I had long ago made my peace. How could I think of Slanderley without bitterness, without recrimination?

The place seldom returned to my waking thoughts. Upon those rare occasions I imagined it without distress. I might be on the back terrace on a summer evening, listening to the comforting roll of the waves below the nearby cliffs. Behind me guests warmly teased and fiddled with one another over cocktails in the hunt room. Another reverie placed me in my favorite chair on a Sunday morning, Scraps by my feet, the *Times* in my lap. I'd glance up to catch my love watching me with her limpid eyes, ones that could melt the hull of a battleship.

Now, awakened by my horrid night's journey, I turned my head to gaze at the calm face of my sleeping love, also freed at last from the treachery of that estate. She had known the secret allure of the spot, tempting as a Venus flytrap. We had almost been swallowed whole, had we not discovered by accident the lethal chemical, as it were, that turned it into a shriveled, unrecognizable corpse.

For our sake, I must end these anxious reminders. I would write my memories down, then burn the result. My psyche needed cremation of this time of my life.

I sighed, sat up, and stared beyond my love's soft form toward the landscape visible beyond the gauze curtains. Semitropical trees danced like waltzing puppets in dawn's early breeze. The sun would soon brighten, so unlike daybreaks of the past. I would not share my dream. Slanderley was no more.

A Quirky Life

Given my nightmare, you must imagine my childhood an unhappy one. Far from it. For one, I was born during the golden Edwardian era. Optimism reigned.

The towers of Slanderley in the background overshadowed our view in the morning. We lived in the stone gate house at the entrance road. This was unusual because my mother, Eleanor Partiger, was head housekeeper, who normally would live in the manor's servant quarters. Her sister, my aunt Jemima, was estate typist, and lived with us as well. My mother adored me as only the parent of a single child would. Being the only male in the household, I felt a protectiveness toward them as women needing a knight, a conviction that rooted in my character.

My mother and her sister had been orphaned at an early age, and lacking relatives willing to take them, ended up in a nasty Victorian orphanage. They left as adolescents to find their own way. Mother joined service at a small estate in Cornwall, yet insisted younger Jemima learn secretarial skills toward a better-paying occupation. In her mid-twenties mother became under-housekeeper at Slanderley, while Jemima filled the vacant secretarial position. Having pulled themselves up, they expected the same from me. I did so, though not as they hoped.

When a toddler, I had the joy of daily outdoors around animals. I recall a day I chased the garden ducks while my mother looked on. Their nipping never frightened me, nor did I cry when I fell down from their chase. When I was older, I headed alone to the stables to watch the grooms care for the horses. Most of the steeds were fine riding specimens, for the Lord of the Manor was an avid huntsman. My favorites however were the large shires with feather-stocking feet that assisted farming chores. These giants handled the heavy plowing and harvesting with grace. My favorite groom was Snerd, a buck-toothed wooden sort who told silly jokes while he combed the horse tails.

Now that I've told you about the manor house, I'm sure you are curious about the larger estate. I'll show you through as though you were a first-time guest being shown about. Taking a side path off the main drive through a copse, we come upon a charming stone cottage overlooking a ravine that ran through the property. A bridge large enough for a horse carriage or car leads over the gorge toward the main house. The cottage intermittently houses visiting designers or lawyers who prefer its privacy to guest rooms in the manor. Surrounded by bays and oaks, it is well-hidden, begging for trysts. Below the bridge are enormous boulders and a vicious run of creek water. Its low wooden guard rails mean we keep away from the edge for fear of falling over. Because the manor house people rarely went on this path, no thought was given to heightening the dangerous guard rail.

As I lead you with caution over the bridge we follow a path back to the main parking circle leading to the grand façade. Though built following the English Civil War, (the 17th century to Yankee readers) Slanderley was saved the accretions of odd additions found at better-known estates. Its broad face hides the two later wings that form the structure into a U. Its stone face is rather austere, with windows placed symmetrically, the only décor being bas relief columns at pleasing intervals and some curious jar-thingies along the top edge of the flat roof.

Some visitors say this façade resembles Highgrove house, owned by the Duchess of Cornwall and the Prince of Wales. Not so! Slanderley is much longer and much older and much bigger. Highgrove is a piddly imitation, some say resembling its owners. Certainly Corwallagagians would agree, for we remain under their curious and questionable control. We a duchy, not a shire. But I digress, so back to the tour.

From here we slip around to a smooth dirt pathway that wanders through an informal garden area. You note the usual sculptures of unidentifiable classical priapic gods and busty goddesses. The plantings are an attempt to look "natural," the design of Terrance Terratigan, a botanist of major minor note.

We come through some trees to arrive at a cliff overlooking a small lagoon. A stone serpentine path invites us to wander down, but I warn you to take a walking stick from the barrel for stability. (Twelve pounds at the gift shop for your very own stick to take home.) We slip and slide down to rest beside a dilapidated wooden boat shack. I lie and say it is two hundred years old, when it was built to look that way by Lord Sinjin for one of his hermits. A boat sits upside down for quick rescues from the treacherous seas.

We enter a nearby stone cottage, which has two cozy rooms decorated with old furnishings appropriate for a damp area. No one lives here, so it invites the fantasies of a child, a readymade play house. As you might guess, this was a focus of my own play on rainy days. I'd don my mackintosh and galoshes to slide down the slippery stone path to the cottage, where I could set a fire and watch the roiling sea from the windows.

Siding the lagoon are two small humps of land resembling lingering elephants. Heading to the right, we clamber a path up toward the backside of the main house. From here the land spreads out to include the practical areas of the estate: kitchen garden, stables, bird pens, dog pens, ice house, silage barn, brewery, workingmen's cottages, and more. Beyond are acres for the long-haired cattle and dairy cows along with fields for hunt runs. As will be evident, many colorful characters oversee this section of the grounds. Though little educated, they are wise in their practical pursuits. Being a boy, I gravitated toward these fellows rather than visit the dowdy house servants in the downstairs kitchen and staff dining room. That is, unless the cook, Mrs. Viscous, was making hot pentacle buns.

Before our tour ends, I finish with a history. Being so isolated, Slanderley must be self-sufficient. Though the house is electrified, storms lead to frequent outages. The nearby village, Slyme Gurney, houses married staff and craftsmen to service the surrounding area. Beyond the main estate acreages sit small holdings whose families center their social life at the village. Unlike today, 1944, a train spur connects to Exeter for the main line for London. When I was younger, such travel was both comfortable and convenient. Still, the estate was nonetheless far enough away that aristocracy did not often include it within their weekend travel plans. As a result, life at Slanderley was not one where the latest fads or fancies mattered.

As for the owners, the story is complicated. During the English Civil War brought about by Oliver Cromwell and the Parliamentarians, many in Cornwall were fast committed to the Royalist cause. As a result, once the monarchy returned, some of its citizens benefitted. James I, a man of literature and theology, settled the beginnings of Slanderley upon Lucas Treconthick, a poet whose religious turns pleased the king. Lucas's wife Nasturtia brought a large dower sufficient to build what composes front of today's house. Nasturtia was also pious and spent much of her time adding rocks to a pile south of the estate. It is now known as Tintagel. Naturally she named her only child Arthur.

The Treconthick line died out, possibly as a result of grandson Launcelot's syphilis. A male cousin inherited, but he died without issue. He was gathering sea shells on the beach when an earthquake in Lisbon caused the great tsunami of 1755.

The house survived but was vacant while interminable court cases ensued as to identifying the proper heir. Enter the de Loverlys, who somehow convinced the probate judges of their due over other claimants. Their name suggests an origin in Norman France, yet I was never able to track their origins. Anyone familiar with the lunatic probate court of the past, *viz.* Dickens's *Bleak House*, will appreciate how some unscrupulous families could unfairly win an estate.

Even the de Loverlys were surprised by the hordes of money hidden in the cellar dungeon by the penurious Treconthicks. They invested it in Cornwall tin mines, and became so rich that they added the large wings as well as absorbed considerable surrounding acreage to form today's estate. Along the way one Treconthick acquired a title, though the reasons are clouded and admittedly suspect.

When the tin mines began to fail, the de Loverlys turned to marriage as a source of wealth. Sinjin (Saint John) was among the first aristocrats to pluck a wife from the States, where money spread among the children, not just to firstborn sons. In 1850 he brought back Peony Van Rockenastor. Accustomed to comfort, his Peony saw to modern changes as they developed, from gas light and electricity to good heating. Out went shabby décor, now priceless Jacobean and Georgian furniture, to be replaced by silks and gilded French seating. She allowed the men their dark den, and arranged the long gallery where chinless ancestors peered down from the walls.

That said, Slanderley's understated elegance disguises the eccentricity of family life. Sinjin kept hermits. He had read of

18th century landowners, like John Timbs of Lancashire, who hired ornamental hermits. These were to live on the estate and appear as venerable bearded men to entertain guests with their eccentricity, or less often be a companion to the landowner.

Sinjin used his artistic bent to design curious hermitages for his eccentrics. One was a Cotswold stone pyramid whose golden hues glittered in the sun. Another was an immense hedgehog structure, its main entrance in the rear. Sinjin's favorite hermit lived the reproduction of a favorite snuff box, with a top that popped up to bring in the sun on the rare days it appeared. The truth is Sinjin's hermits had frequent company, namely the Lord himself, for entertainments not to be discussed further.

Lady Peony was only too happy to leave him to his hobbies so she could indulge her own. Superior now to her old friends across the Atlantic, she took up roaming the Blessed Isle by foot. Her intent was to hit as many public houses as possible and snooker the darts players out of their pounds. The game was one she mastered during childhoods at Fifth Avenue and Newport mansions. She needed the money because she early discovered Sinjin took total patriarchal control of her dower. Her parents' American lawyers neglected that such could occur, so she needed pin money to buy herself fresh panties.

Lady Peony did not neglect her duty. She first bore a daughter, Euphoria, and years later the heir, Leo. But Peony came from a long line of screwballs, one more bonkers than coursing the de Loverly blood. Consequently she arrived one day from a very successful cross-country hike riding a sheep she insisted was her cousin Rudolph. Once Lord Sinjin noticed the sheep at the dinner table, where it had sat for a number of weeks, he sent Lady Peony to a convent for protection. There she died soon after of some rare cloven-hoof animal virus.

Sinjin passed away soon afterward, of a broken heart. He truly missed the fey Peony, for she had done so well at darts that she added much to estate coffers.

Euphoria oversaw the care of her brother so well that he took to calling her "Nan" and demanded his real nanny be fired. Nan shaped Leo toward his baronial duties. She sent him to a public boarding school (private, to Yanks) where any hints of artiness or sensitivity were pounded out of him. Lacking intellectual prowess, he returned to accept his main assignment: find a rich wife to produce and heir and spare. Nan searched abroad and found Gladys Van Rockenastor, a second cousin. The family was happy to be rid of her because she had six toes on one foot. It is unclear whether Leo ever noticed such.

Leo wasn't quite a dim wit, but so retiring he gave that impression. Despite having two certifiable parents, he was placid and easily satisfied. He quickly absorbed the requirements of his status, which resulted in regular trips to London to enjoy the fellowship of his club, and to pursue a full hunt season. Alas his wife Gladys was no saner than Lady Peony. She bore a son, Algernon, a daughter, Letitia. To everyone's shock, Peony announced her desire to convert to Catholicism. Soon

```
              SLANDERLEY OWNERSHIP
                    JAMES II
                 grants lands to
         Lucas TRECONTHICK m. Nasturtia ?
                        |
           Arthur T. m. Jujube Barnswog
                        |
           Rupert T. m. Geneva Ooocham
                        |
               Launcelot T. [no issue]
                 Cousin inherits
                 Lucas T. [no issue]
                        |
                 Estate in Probate
                        |
                 Still in Probate
                        |
           Phineas DE LOVERLY m. Doris Cheese
                        |
              Philo deL. m. Philomena Nog
                        |
        Saint John (Sinjin) deL. m. Peony Van Rockenastor
        |----------------------------------|
   Leo deL m. Gladys Van Rockenastor    Euphoria (Nan)
                                              |
                       Algernon----------Letitia
```

she was found smashed on the rocks beneath the stone bridge, a circumstance that led to local gossip concerning the cause.

This last event occurred when I was about five and able to poke about the estate on my own. Most interesting to me were the two children a few years younger than I. Sometimes I encountered them at play, but being a son of service, I was not invited inside the manor. They little interested me anyway. Used to being on my own from an early age, I preferred roaming about and peeking into estate activities, chatting with the games keeper, gardeners, grooms and others. I had a fairyland for my imagination, which dominated my thoughts and led to fanciful stories.

Algie's appearance was typical of the de Loverlys—curly ginger hair, small green eyes, and a small cleft chin. Letty took after their deceased mother's line—straight dark hair, blue eyes, and lantern jaw. From an early age they preferred the outdoors, tumbling about with their spaniels. As soon as Letty could hold a tennis racket, Algie taught her the game. His style was one of smashing balls directly at her body. She seemed curiously unaffected by his attacks, nor did she mind his wrestling her face into mud. She was a hearty, good-natured girl.

At outdoor events, I noticed Algie hang along the sidelines, eyes cast down to avoid contact with another person. When an elderly visitor asked how he was, Algie would mumble and twist his body about as though squeezing out his words. He'd ask to be excused early and dash off into the woods, perhaps to seek out a snakeskin for his collection. Letitia on the other hand was the gushing sort who sparkled in company and assumed everyone would love her.

The children's lives were regimented by the demands of strict comportment and dress. Their Scottish nannies competed to see who was sterner. "She made me take cold baths," revealed Letitia later, "while Algie was forced to sit in the snow and wash his face with it." Being heir, he had the harder path. Whereas Letitia had basic schooling from age eight, Algie faced a tutor from age three to prepare him for later elite public schools. At age seven he left for one of the notorious boys' boarding schools, Darnford, where brutality ruled in the schoolroom and lodgings. Each holiday he returned a bit more withdrawn and sullen. (I attended the local in Slyme Gurney, of course.)

When I was about eight, Letitia approached me one day as I was watching their outdoor bowls game and asked if I would like to join them. I hesitated, but she insisted. Algie just nodded his chin in agreement when I looked over. Being naturally clumsy, I readily lost to both, which placed me in Algie's favor. Though we three were hardly close friends, we developed separate agreeable relationships.

During his school breaks I boosted Algie's timidity by marching him farther afield on the estate. I taught him how to warn the cattle of our approach so they would not charge, and which berries were edible. He often brought his rifle to shoot at hares or wild birds. Hunting was his element. He preferred the stalking in contrast to organized fox hunts or grouse shoots. He was usually taciturn, yet spoke to me almost as an equal. I felt sorry he was forced into a cruel educational tradition.

Only secondhand information suggested Algie was more complex than I believed. Working in Slanderley, Aunt Jemima observed his behavior there. She said he threw fits during Letitia's birthdays, demanding he receive identical presents.

One day he was found trimming the whiskers off the cats, and a maid came screaming out of his room over the sight of a badger carcass in his bed. Jemima took these and others as worrisome signs, where my mother insisted he was just a boy, that his actions were not unusual. I sided with my mother, for unknown to her I did some nasties with local frogs and threw my own fits.

Letitia was more playful. She made the fisherman's cottage into her private space for make-believe encounters. By age eleven she had several friends from her all-girl day school who visited for weekends of charades and pantomimes. Being the only male, I was the Prince in the stories to her Princess. She insisted on cuddling and kissing me. Her girlfriends teased me for my curly hair and sparkling lapis eyes. In adolescence she entertained mixed groups, though I was no longer welcome. Yet she often sought me out if she noticed me on the lawn or by the lagoon and came over for a chatty conversation. Almost as tall as I, she'd suggest a snog, this time more seriously. My response was to blush, turn, and run off.

One other family member made frequent acquaintance. She was Lord Leo's Aunt Euphoria. She had spent some years at art school in London and traveling abroad. By the time she settled in at Slanderley she was unwed and insisted we all call her Nan. "Algernon called me Nan, for I was more his mother than his real one, and older as well." (Not to mention sane, I'd think to myself.)

Nan was born with a happy gene, and always looked on the bright side of life. She broke the strict rules between service and family, much to the humiliation of the butler, Bunston. Sometimes she even ate below stairs or asked Cook if she could watch how a dish was prepared. She was a wicked rider, the best in the duchy, and known to have the keenest eye at horse sales. Her short height and feminine style belied a determined independent soul. She lived apart from the family in the West Wing, which was closest to the ocean.

Nan's favorite staff member was Aunt Jemima, which led to her visiting us often for tea. She always arrived in flowing bright colors, a feathered hat whispering in the breeze, a bouquet in her arms. Once settled, she'd call me over to sit beside her and would ask me about my day's adventures. For birthdays she gave me gifts beyond my mother's reach, such as a large toy sail boat to race in the pond against Algie's, or a full collection of Hardy novels. When I was eleven, she brought a gramophone and taught me to dance the waltz, which I never conquered. She also recounted dramatic stories of the manor's history, of which you shall soon learn.

The lack of a father never troubled me. With two loving women and Nan to watch over me, I did not miss siblings either. I admit to being spoiled, and in some ways became entitled to getting what I wanted. Yet living in such a wondrous setting, with so much to entrance me, I desired little.

What really set my life's purpose was the village school. I discovered the wonder of books. The village teacher delighted in having a pupil so entranced with words. She gave me a used dictionary to keep and introduced me to the small town library. Aware of the latter's inadequacies, she lent books of her own, thus exposed me to the classics normally taught at boys' public schools. By age ten I was parsing Latin to the neglect of arithmetic. As a result, my bookishness reinforced my solitary temperament. Living on the estate, I had adults for companions. Praised by mother, aunt, and teachers, I also gained self-confidence, which expressed itself in a commanding, somewhat superior demeanor. I believed myself so much better off than my classmates, a Lord in my own mind.

Clarice Stasz

A Birthday Surprise

An unexpected command appearance early set my life's course. On my 14th birthday, Lord Leo de Loverly required I attend him in his library at Slanderley. This message unnerved me. First, I had never before spoken to the man, though of course I saw him about the estate grounds on horseback or with guns headed for some pheasant shoot. Although he was not a frightening sort, quite the opposite, I did not know his true temperament. Second, I expected he was to send me away now that I was of age for such removal.

Having little acquaintance beyond the service wing, I crept in wonder through the long portrait hall searching for the appointed room. Images of ginger-haired chinless ancestors stared sternly, scowled at my intrusion. At the north end I discovered a smaller hall, one door open upon a two-storied room clad in floor-to-ceiling bookcases, a winding staircase leading to the balcony level volumes.

Lord Leo was by the hearth, a large map in his hands. When he noticed me peeking around the doorway, he encouraged me to enter. He was dressed like a tweedy squire, his hand grasping feather quill. His face revealed nothing of what was to come, so my hands began to shake and I stood back at the door.

"Here, Edmund, don't tarry. You're a man now. Come here, that's right, sit there across from me. I must discuss your future. Fourteen is the age for making plans. Now, tell me, what would you want most in the world, if you could have it?"

"Why, sir, just to stay at Slanderley. That is enough for me."

"What an odd response. You don't want travel and adventure in foreign lands?" He turned the map toward me and pointed his quill at the Indian Ocean. "Perhaps join the King's Navy?"

"No, sir."

"Not hundreds and hundreds of pounds, a treasure chest?"

"No, sir, I'm content here at Slanderley." I shook my head ferociously to emphasize my point.

"By that, I suppose you mean to live like Algernon, lord of the manor, so to speak." He hinted at a wry smile.

"Not at all, sir, though I would like to read your books. And be in service."

"Most people would call you a fool, Edmund. Certainly your half-brother would think so."

My eyes opened wide. My half-brother? Algernon?

"Now don't give me that look of surprise. We both know I am your father. Given your ginger hair you would be a true fool not to have deduced such by now. And your answer convinces me I am indeed your father to have such a wise son, not like Algernon, so dull, like his sad late mother. At least he hasn't become a Papist."

I tried to control a laugh while he continued.

"But tell me why my first-born son rejects obvious opportunities. By rights, had your mother not been downstairs maid, could I have married her, you would be at public school now. Indeed, I could still offer you such benefice."

"Well, sir---"

"You may call me father now, in private."

"Father---"

"Good!" He relit his pipe and leaned back in his chair.

"If recognized as a de Loverly, I should have to go to balls and I hate to dance. I should have to visit with people like the Bishop and his wife, who, forgive my impudence, sir, stuff themselves like pigs at picnics while proclaiming the poor are blessed and should make the best of their starvation. And the hunts, where I differ so from you, seem so cruel to me, even though the riders are such poor aims that they usually miss the foxes. It's the spirit behind me that disturbs me, the heaving a weapon at furry little creatures and feathered friends."

"Humph, I see we shall need to discuss the delights of the hunt another time. But 'impudence,' where'd you get a vocabulary like that?"

"My teachers lend me books because I am far ahead of the class. That's why I would stay at Slanderley, where I could have quiet and time to read."

Lord Leo frowned, "Too bad, Edmund. I was hoping to educate you for a place in Civil Service, for a life of comfort in London. Your intelligence suggests a valuable contribution to that ignorant body. Are you sure that doesn't interest you? There are wonderful libraries in the city."

"No, sir, er, father. I've read enough of such lives not to wish one. I am spoiled. I want to be a country man with few distractions and few responsibilities. I do not envy Algernon at all." I was beginning to sense a catch of confidence.

"A harsh critic of yourself too? Well, Edmund, I shall arrange what you desire. First, I will see that you are welcome to use my library whenever Algernon is not around. Next, I shall put you in training for service here. You will start at the bottom, but my goal is to see you as butler within few years. I'll confide in Bunston to ensure that he gives you the finest preparation to replace his retirement. His brandy recipes must survive. Finally, I shall advise my solicitors of our relationship to enter you accordingly in my will, namely your permanent status at Slanderley."

Astonished by this news, I rose to run toward my father to take his hand. He put his palm up to stop my progress.

"Not so fast. You must make a solemn oath to me in return. Promise me you will never disclose your relationship to Algernon. Taking as he does after his dear demented mother, he could not bear the humiliation. He needs to enjoy his fantasy of manor life, more a caricature than reality, to feel secure and less likely to bring harm through his duties."

His frank commentary surprised me, as did his request. "I'm unclear, sir. Can you explain?"

"Think this way. Algernon is shy and basically loving underneath, but I worry his school is producing a bully. I was able to fight that tendency myself, though I fear he lacks the self-confidence to do so. Our best approach is to—as you would say—spoil him."

"Not frustrate, you mean."

"Correct! Now come here, lad, and shake my hand to seal the bargain. Later I shall ask Dr. Phlew to draw blood, but a shake of hand will suffice for now. Now tell me about your favorite writers."

Following a brief discussion of Dickens, for I knew Lord Leo read his works, I verily skipped out of the room. Rather than go directly home, I wandered into the downstairs reception hall and adjoining salons. I was tempted to visit the private family apartments in the East Wing yet held back. When I was to live in Slanderley it would be downstairs among the staff. At the green baize door leading to the servant stairwell I caught an aroma of the family's next meal, duck in orange sauce mixing with freshly baked bread and turnips.

When I returned home, both my mother and Aunt Jemima surprised me as well with a large cake and a wardrobe suited for a man. They knew of my visit with Lord Leo and tittered with glee that now they no longer need keep the secret of my origins from me.

"Why did you do so?" I fretted. "You could have told me years ago."

"Leo made me promise," explained my mother, "that he would take care of you when you came of age, no matter what happened to me. But he wanted to be the one to tell you."

"Yes, he was very kind," I responded, "but how horrible for you to stay here while you could not marry. How cruel he was."

"One day you will better understand, Eddie. Have I seemed unhappy?" She walked over and took my hand. "I enjoy a good life. A much better one that were I to go off to another manor to work. And here too has my sister shared my joy."

I banged on the large atlas they had just given me, for I was too immature to be other than furious. "Well don't expect me to believe you. And he might be my father—"

"Shush, Eddie. He is shy and kind. Please accept any of his offers to join him from now on. I insist."

Growling, I rushed out of the cottage without even discussing details of my conversation with Lord Leo. I went down to the beach, where I found Letitia leaning against the gunwale of a boat. She gave a toothy smile and patted the side for me to sit beside her.

"Oh, Eddie, it is such a lovely day this weather." (She meant drizzle instead of downpour.) No more school. No more books. I can do anything I want all summer."

"And what is that?"

"I can ride to Slyme Gurney and sneak some lemon drink at the pub. Sit in the snug away from the villagers and meet a girlfriend. Chitchat, you know."

"Oh, that's right, you are now twelve. What special gift did you receive?"

"My pick of a new rider at the next horse fair and a telephone for the house. The latter took a lot of begging. Pater is so old-fashioned that way. It will be put in a side room by the cloak closet. So it is private even though it is not just for me."

"I wonder if he will set one in the lodge house now, so my mother and Aunt Jemima can make and take calls to yours. It would be so convenient for everyone."

"Not likely, knowing Pater. He was in such a good mood at lunch. It's too bad you don't know him."

I smiled to myself and my mind wandered while she went on about the horse she hoped to own. I knew I would have to see Lord Leo soon and ask for the lodge telephone.

I did so some weeks later when he requested another visit. This time Bunston was present. That man, still very healthy in his late fifties, was clearly hesitant about the possibility of my replacing him at retirement. When Lord Leo referred to an excellent pension upon departure, Bunston warmed to the secret training he must provide once I entered service. That change was put off until my fifteenth birthday. Lord Leo suggested I use the year freely, that I had a heavy life ahead of me.

Until then Lord Leo, for I could not think of him as otherwise, saw me every few weeks. He walked me through the long hall and spoke about the ancestral figures. He took me to the amazing trophy room filled with antlers of every size and shape, along with stuffed birds and small mammals. It was a veritable miniature Pitt Rivers Museum. I was revolted by the evidence of kills, a meagre number representing several centuries of slaughter, yet I held silent while he admired the specimens and reminisced over his own catches. Another time he showed me the gun cabinets, one near the cloak closet, another within the trophy room. He insisted I learn gun cleaning and handling and made me accompany him on some rabbit hunts. I did so for his pleasure, a small payment for my future's guarantee. I pretended to be a poor aim, to his dismay. In truth I was born with exceptional vision.

When I went to the library to borrow a Thucydides, Plato, or *Daddy Darwin's Dovecote*, he insisted I sit and read in the far corner while he went about his work. I realized he wished me to overhear his conversations with key staff so I could appreciate the immensity of the estate and its management. I learned of problems involving the stables or the fields. Aunt Jemima came to take down letters for his lawyers and accountants. I realized I was being educated in topics Algernon must later acquire.

Whenever my mother entered, she curtsied, then sat nearby, quite against expectation. They'd whisper together so I could not hear their plans involving secret meetings at the Pyramid hermitage.

My formal schooling had ended, so I continued my habit of self-improvement. I grew tall and gained muscles by assisting for fun in the stable, whether mucking a stall or grooming a shire. I learned to swim in the lagoon, and unusual skill at a time even fishermen drowned for lack of such. Despite such athleticism, I retained a mild clumsiness in fine movement. The one exception was darts, which I played at the Earless

Coachman in the village, and won many a shilling. There was proof of my heritage, Lady Peony's one valuable skill.

Fascinated by history, I decided upon an extended trip from Exeter to Plymouth. Once arriving in that city by train, I explored the Roman remains and bits of wall. The Cathedral's immensity left me feeling like a pismire. Its astronomical clock left me wondering over the minds able to construct such a wonder. I had never been to a city before, and found the new electric trams frightening, yet the electric lights on the High Street calmed my fears of walking there at night. I provisioned myself at its stores and prepared for a trek of over a hundred miles.

My plan was a dangerous tramp through the moors to locate remnants of the tin industry that grew Slanderley's wealth. Given the unpredictable fog on those windswept heights, it was easy to lose one's bearings. Of the notorious bogs, I almost made a precarious entry, but caught my footing in time. Tales of men on horseback leaving only their hats as signs of the sucking, mud-drowning death were true.

I stayed one night in Princetown, the closest village to terrifying Dartmoor Prison. Its appearance matched its horrid reputation, a brutal rain-scarred dark-stoned monster. Only some sheep foraging in the foreground fields softened the image. That night a tree's scratching at my window woke me up in fear an escaped murderer was outside.

The next day full of sun, I could hike away quickly to study stone remnants of circular huts built four millennia earlier. My imagination filled them with pelt-covered families around a hearth. Were the moor ponies here back then? Or had they dinosaurs? I needed to read more science and less mythology or fiction. I came upon medieval crosses and pilgrim pathways, along with longhouses still used by farmers. The moors deserved to haunt visitors, not just for their curious geology, but for all the life the seemingly vacant acreage covered. No wonder Cornwall attracts frightening myths.

Upon my return from a jaunty stay in Plymouth, I took my new place at Slanderley. I moved into the manor, serving as sub-sub-footman, where I quickly graduated from carrying letters on trays to sticking stamps on them. I graduated to the silver room, which meant I carried one key. My next service as footman was brief. I had yet to control my gangly body and decorated more than one dinner guest with claret and mash. My favorite chore was learning to make squashes and cordials from fruit and berries. One day Bunston caught me experimenting with cuckoo pint berries. Had he not stopped me, the dinner table would have turned into a vomitorium.

By now Lord Leo and Nan were the only constant residents. Algernon continued to board at his school, while Letitia left for hers early each day. She often took fortnight visits within her social circle, to the Hampshires or the Cotswolds. Apart from one of Lord Leo's old friends appearing for tea, little socializing occurred. Limited chores freed me considerable time to be in the library, where I learned repair of ancient books, and read them in the process.

Part of my rapid advance was due to staff leaving for war and munition factories. At its height during Victoria's reign,

Slanderley's retinue was a complex hierarchy of positions, with an ordering of maids, from lady's maid to scullery, footmen and house boys, gardeners, stable keeper and stud manager, games keeper and boat man. Very much an outdoor family, the de Loverlys granted Masters of the Hunt and Hounds special privileges. The staff gradually reduced during the tenure of Lady Peony. Her wanderings meant fewer balls, fancy dinners, and charity fetes so demanding of help.

However immodest it sounds, I was so efficient and agreeable that I became a pet for the staff, notably the women, who clung to me all the more as they watched their nephews, brothers, husbands, and boyfriends leave for the slaughter of WWI. They taught me lessons no book can instruct, and I was always a willing pupil, who became most accomplished, to their delight.

Mourning

WWI's devastation escaped Algernon, who hid securely in some obscure London government office that Lord Leo had arranged. Algie joined other sole surviving heirs there, one of those aristocratic sanctities hidden from the public. They carried official cards hinting at top secret work to protect them when accosted for not being overseas. In truth the protection saved the war front from yet another group of incompetent officers.

That safety was not so for several male staff, whose bodies returned too soon after departure to be placed in the Slyme Gurney churchyard. Apart from one who died in a munitions factory explosion, the women survived their contributions. Yet few returned, having found their newfound independence and exposure to a wider world more attractive than service on a most isolated estate. (Some years afterward I encountered one serving as a greeter at an Exeter legal firm.)

Lord Leo was much troubled by the horrendous death toll and spent his breakfast chittering over the latest news, angry he was helpless to change anything. To calm himself, in the afternoons he leapt upon his fastest steed and pressed through the countryside with such speed as to suggest a death wish. And so one day his horse tripped, tossing my dear father head-first into a stone wall and instant death. I had to break the news to my mother, who grew inconsolable over the loss of her great love.

Algernon returned from London for the funeral and served with dignity. Yet when I entered his room several days later, I observed a large grin on his face, unable to squelch the delight of his new status as Lord de Loverly. He now retained the emotional coolness required of his class as a defense. Letitia was closer to her father, and secretly teary. Still, while meeting the mourners, she skimmed the men for potential marital prospects.

I was called in as one of the pall bearers, along with Bunston, a terrible task in that I had to subdue my grief. After the burial I begged illness to stay with my mother and Aunt Jemima, the only location the three of us could speak openly of our losses.

When the war ended in 1918 we were still in mourning. Death continued its march in a new form, the Spanish flu pandemic. Although it struck hardest on young adults, my mother was too weakened from grief and succumbed within three days. She settled in a grave within view of Lord Leo's, not quite joined with him in eternity.

Upon my mother's death, Nan called me in for a private talk in her West Wing apartment. She sat by the hearth swathed in layers of black silk and jet jewelry. Cadbury the Persian snuggled in her lap. Following the obligatory talk of the weather, she dove into her purpose.

"You must understand how Lord Leo suffered as a child. His father was off buggering hermits while his mother was going mad. I was young and wanted my own fun, so I hurried him off to a boarding school too early. Only later did I realize he needed a mother figure and returned for his vacations. He had a sweet nature, but little chance to enjoy life as he could.

"It was no surprise when I came to visit and discovered Leo watching your mother with googly eyes. I had to step in. The family name had been damaged enough by my brother and his wife. I couldn't allow Leo to wed a common house maid."

"Common! My mother was not common."

"You're right—I'm sorry. I only mean that is how society would consider her. She was far from common in her sensibilities. But she had no blood line. Then we found out she was pregnant, and Leo was ready to elope to India if necessary. That would mean another nasty probate among the distant cousins."

"Which means you would no longer live at Slanderley. So you selfishly—"

"Selfishly locked him up. Yes, I did think of myself as well as the family. I called his godfather, Lord Woodchamp, to talk sense into Leo. After several weeks in the dungeon he submitted to his future. He agreed to Gladys as his wife and enough bonking to produce an heir. In return, your mother filled a position in the de Loverly London townhouse for safe keeping until you were a year old. Any staff in the know were paid off. We all agree your mother would return to live in the lodge and become house keeper."

"And meanwhile my father wed beautiful, pious Gladys."

"Yes, though I wish your mother could have been at the altar. Instead he ended up with that inbred North American, not that her money didn't help redo the roof. But I've always believed there's some Yorkist blood somewhere back."

"Or worse, Welsh," I added. We each shivered like Eskimos over that thought. Once I opened some elderberry wine we turned to lighter topics.

Nan's maid Rose entered. "I apologize for interrupting. Mr. Quirk, can you please help me with a problem in my hearth grate?"

After excusing myself, I followed her to discover her problem was a feint. She thought I needed some special comfort to soften my grief. After our spooning I wandered through the thick fog to the gatehouse, where Aunt Jemima was packing my mother's clothes.

"Eddie, I will stay on as secretary for a bit, but it is time I leave these sad memories. Your mother would want me to go to the city, which has always been my dream. You are a grown man now and no longer need my interfering tendencies."

"I shall miss you terribly, Aunt, but perhaps you will find a brighter future there. Maybe even a husband."

She paused and sat down. "Actually that is a possibility. I have had a correspondence with a Mr. Titmouse. He has a gardening business and could use a woman with business experience. Since inquiring about the position, we have discovered our shared interest in training hedgehogs."

"So you have a job—and more. I am so happy for you, Aunt. I hope to walk you down an aisle one day."

She came over to hug me. "I'm sure it will be very soon."

Given her intended departure, I too began to pack for a move into the servant quarters. The change stimulated my imagination. What paper for the walls? What antique furniture could I pull out of the unused West Wing chambers? Given the shortage of staff, I could add doors to connect a sitting room, wardrobe, and bedroom. Such impertinence would be cause for eviction elsewhere, but Aunt Jemima would see to the expense covered under another category.

I headed back to Slanderley for afternoon bacchanals. Mrs. Viscous, Bunston, and I drank brandies and reminisced. When Bunston heard of my plans to move into the manor, he announced he would retire to resettle in Ceylon. It appeared he too had a marriage in mind, to a widowed house keeper on a tea plantation, a sweetheart from his youth.

At that time I was Algernon's valet. He expressed a curious preoccupation with leather, his main concern that his boots be well-oiled. Lackadaisical in his personal grooming, I could have dressed him in the same shirt for a week and he wouldn't have noticed. Truth is I did so one time, but Bunston gave me a sharp dressing down.

"Only artists and geniuses can dress as fools", he advised. "If you attire Algernon in eccentric dress, people will treat him accordingly. Dress him sharp, Eddie, and save everyone a heap of confusion."

I became such a meticulous groom of Algernon's clothes and person that he became known for his outstanding finish. I was familiar with the angle of each rebellious hair on his chin. He had a perpetual hangnail on his left pinkie requiring special care.

While I oversaw him, he'd sit sullenly, barking intermittent blather from his vertiginous stream of consciousness: falling trout populations, a new gizmo for the sports car, cricket matches, tricks played on friends. Nary a word about girls. In other words, he was developing a character typical of men of his breeding. When socializing, he draped louche against a mantel, a cigarette flicked more than smoked, his lush ginger hair haloed by the fire.

Were it not for the astute solicitors in the city, Slanderley might have swirled into a spiral of destruction. Immediately following his father's death, Algernon returned home yet seemed lost over what to do with his time. So long as his needs were met, he little interfered in our lives. It was for house servants like being on holiday, while the outdoors men ran the fields and livestock as they knew best.

Once the year of mourning for his father ended, Algie surprised us all by leaving. He joined one of London's esteemed banking houses, a harmless niche for well-bred men known to be less than competent. It was like MI6, always welcoming "the right sort," whether capable or not. He returned only for local hunts, and otherwise ignored decisions concerning the estate. With Jemima off, they remained now in my hands.

Letitia was another matter. While the probate was being settled, temporary budget reductions left her wailing over the diminishment of her clothing allowance. She used any pretext to fill the house with chattering friends for picnics on the beach, dinners followed by charades, and rehearsals of pantomimes for special evenings when her friends' parents also visited.

I felt sorry for her, orphaned and adrift at the time she most needed a woman's wise counsel. Lacking beauty, she made up for it through social grace and essential kindness. Her constant prattle, while annoying to me, was taken to be evidence of intelligence among her status. She was well-set for her future as the lady of some other man's manor.

Once I ascended butler, Letty believed I would indulge her wishes more freely. She was right, save for one. She'd sneak up behind me in a hall and throw her arms around from behind to startle my stern demeanor.

'Oh, Quirk, you're so much more handsome than the boys I know."

She'd run her hand through my sumptuous locks. While I pushed that hand out, the other slipped inside my waistcoat, causing no small arousal.

"If only you weren't a servant, I'd—"

"Please, my lady! I take your comment merely as a tease. I expect you will soon be laughing about it with your friends."

Then I'd enumerate the virtues of Boy Sexsmith and Newby Newcomp, frequent visitors.

She'd stop, pout, sigh, and wander off. Once I overheard her cry to the heir to the Earl of Sexsmith that *I* had approached *her* in an unseemly manner. He suggested they go to one of the hermitages so he "could make it up to her." She declined and later threw her virginity in my face.

In general I appreciated Letty's presence, her livening up the household, and was pained I could not share that she was my half-sister. In 1920 she married a virtuous youth and heir to a mere baron, Reginald Horsham. A similarly toothy fellow, he shared her country bent for fast horses and the breeding of hounds. How I missed the scatter of girlish magazines in the morning room, the whoops of laughter as she chased the dogs into the lilacs, the array of clothes on the floor when I brought in mail during her breakfast.

Other changes exacerbated my position. When I advertised for a house keeper to replace my mother, experienced replacements soon complained about the location and the lack of sufficient maids. This led to a revolving door. I had to remake several rooms into a commodious apartment like my own to keep Mrs. Viscous cooking. Only a few older staff remained, mainly the men in charge of various outside duties, such as Willets, Widgeon, Snerd, and Sloth.

I now phoned London representatives to oversee estate legal formalities, yet I knew we needed a business manager on site. That was not within my realm, however. I despaired of the long-term viability of Slanderley. Magnificent homes were being dynamited, and land turned over developers. Being in Cornwall protected us for the nonce, yet I fretted for my future. I wasn't equipped to make investment decisions, let alone which crops to plant where. Slanderley could collapse were it to remain in my control.

Clarice Stasz

A Saviour Returns

Algernon returned for good in 1922. His bank's Board of Directors found him beyond their very liberal tolerance for incompetence. He was not so much asked to leave as encouraged to trade in finance, for which he had little predilection, for the country. I imagine a director saying, "Lord Algernon, you must continue the vaunted traditions crumbling all around us. You are in a unique position to serve a *noble cause* on the nation's behalf."

Grabbing that mantle, he obsessed over now-lost practices. For example, he designed calling cards and insisted on the archaic tradition concerning corner-folding by visitors. This meant only the most addlepated residents around Slyme Gurney graced the tea table and dining room. Such boors fawned around Algernon like starved piglets to a diffident sow.

Unlike his chinless ancestry, he was taut and fit from sport. Since he seldom spoke, others assumed he was overly thoughtful. Thanks to my training his new valet, he remained known for his impeccable style and trim. *Town and Country* profiled him a wise aristocrat. Let's be frank: for an isolated region in need of romantic myths and events, an orangutan could have been cast in role of local benefactor had it half Algie's hauteur.

SLANDERLEY

Adding to tradition, he sent Nan to live in Chilsworth, a large, damp-stained house surrounded by nettled fields and sloppy seasonal ponds. "There can be only one person in charge," he asserted, "and I as sole heir and son must ensure my sovereignty."

It was not unusual for a wife or other relative to be sent off following the death of the prominent male. Histories abound with young heirs evicting their mothers to small demesnes. It was cruel nonetheless. Thus it was a mournful day I saw her off with her devoted maid Rose. At least I could visit both in their marshy dell on the estate's southern border.

Then Algie changed his office to the trophy room. In addition to hunt kills mentioned earlier, it sported Victorian Age collections. Nothing was too small to be preserved, from a lizard to a beetle. Dominating the ceiling was a chandelier of red deer antlers. Mothy bits of exotica from other parts of the world suggested the travels of previous de Loverlys. With their dead glassy eyes they were perfect companions for Algie, mute and obedient. After breakfast, it was there I met with him to discuss any special orders for the day.

Another cruel order was among his first. "Quirk, those big horses with the fluffy stockings have to go."

"The shires, milord?"

"Yes, and as soon as possible. Why have anything one can't ride during a hunt?"

"The next horse fair is in May. I'll see to their listing."

"Horse fair? I mean today. Shoot them!"

So advised, I rushed off to inform Glum, their groom. He shuttled them off to a small farmer's land to keep until the fair, then returned to give off six shots close enough for Algie to hear.

Often at meetings I offered Algie notions he restated as his demands. Knowing it would economize, I shut off the West Wing now that Nan was gone. Staff closed velvet drapes over shuttered windows, and draped furniture with ghostly shrouds. The two remaining gardeners, Snerd and Sloth, attended primarily to the kitchen garden and floral displays close to the manor. The forester having left, the trees along the long entrance drive cowered over to shadow and scrape the arriving automobiles.

Algie himself discovered the motor car, and preferred to speed about in his sportster rather than be chauffeured in the limousine. He bought a Rolls Royce 40/50, later to be replaced by a Morgan Super Aero. Thanks to the light population of the duchy, he never killed anyone, though he took his share of rooks and rabbits feeding on the single tracks roadways.

Among the few events he attended overnight were road races. Because he preferred me serving as valet during these jaunts, I sat beside him, sweat streaming down my back, knees pressed hard together. I foresaw us overturning on a curve, beheading us both. My fears were unjustified, for in becoming athletic at public skill he acquired quick reflexes.

The day came when more drastic measures were needed concerning household staff. I obtained a copy of the recent

SLANDERLEY

Parliamentary Report on Domestic Servants, prepared because the "servant problem," the lack of workers, faced the entire aristocracy and middle class. Finding the conclusions useful, I hinted at its radical ideas in a manner to convince Algernon.

"Excuse me, my Lord. I've been thinking what a waste it is to room and board the maids. Let them be day workers, with only a lunch provided. Widgeon can pick them up and deliver them from the village. Some women who have married might return daily in that case."

"What? Hhmph. Oh, yes, a good idea. Save much money. Why not?"

Another time I noted, "I've been thinking about our housekeeper problem. I can pick up a dandy one with a jack-of-all-trades man were we to offer one of the unused cottages. We needn't feed them either, apart from lunch."

Seeing how well the maid problem was solved, he readily agreed. This resulted in an elderly yet competent couple, Mr. and Mrs. Danderfull. This gnomish pair were of good cheer as well, and further improved the mood of everyone in service.

The final touch was most important to prevent turnover. "About the staff, my lord, I'd suggest a tiny increase in wages and another afternoon off, or perhaps all of Sunday. This ploy will make them feel as respectable as those at Menabilly "

"More than Menabilly? What do you mean? Of course our service is superior to Menabilly and every place else. We are eminently respectable."

"True, but these new servants have been misled by the wireless into thinking wages from a company are more honorable than those from an estate. Foolish of course, but we do want the best people—beat the others at their game, as it were."

"Humph, um, er. Damnation, I don't like it, but you have been correct in the past. But only as an experiment, Quirk, with just a few at first. Only as an experiment."

With these ploys I assembled a small, proud staff that was the envy of guests, who never suspected Algie's solution to "the servant problem." Mrs. Viscous helped by cooking way too much for the evening dinner to serve as the help's luncheon the next day. I included the special cordials Bunston had taught me to stock the servants' lounge at the end of the day.

One of the few decisions Algie made on his own was to hire an estate business manager. Apparently he had met Freddie Wickleworm in the city during a stay at his club. Freddie wasn't a member but was invited by a guest who knew Algie. I later learned Freddie schemed this to worm his way into Algie's graces.

When Freddie arrived, I faced the slender, sinewy build of a ballet dancer. His dimpled smile accompanied a rich baritone voice. His suit was bespoke, the wool an understated thin hand weave. I filed a reminder to learn of his tailor for Algie's next London sartorial venture.

I walked him through the copse to the cottage by the gorge. Having a separate domicile was his one requirement.

Approving its convenient, cozy rooms, I heard him discuss the rearrangement of furniture and placement of his own décor.

"May I ask why you chose this hideaway after the rich pleasures of the city?"

"I didn't want to end up a glorified clerk in a government bureau. Though I attended Oxford, I knew my lack of family importance meant I would never advance. Now I have the best of both worlds: Slanderley, a cottage of my own, the outdoors, and when bored, London, to handle meet financial connections. My goal is to be fully independent in ten years, and I have the brains to achieve such with little effort."

"How can you manage that on an estate salary?"

"Easy. I have convinced Algernon to add a bonus, a percentage of monetary gains. This motivates me to maximize his profits and mine at the same time."

Fortunately, Freddie and I had much in common beyond our cunning and intellectualism. Many free hours we hiked the grounds to compete at twitching. With the coast bordering the estate on the west, we perched on the cliffs to watch passing skuas and shearwaters. We often talked late into the night discussing poetry or politics over Cuban cigars and brandy.

Where we differed soon became evident. Freddie's position involved more than reading stock indices and land purchase regulations. Observing the advisors and salesmen approaching his cottage, I concluded they shared a predilection for a kind of love so tolerated in boys' schools yet condemned among men, what Havelock Ellis called Inversion. Doubtless more than one secret tip reached Freddie's ears during times of private affection.

Freddie's active sexual life only stirred my own. While enamoured of women, marriage and fatherhood never appealed to me. Thus I pledged myself to avoid relations with women of my status, unless like Rose they held no fruitless hopes concerning marriage. Rather, I found charming and willing paramours among unhappy wives about Slyme Gurney, and even titled houseguests. Nor was I fussy as to appearance. Thin or plump, young or old, gorgeous or plain, all they need express was willingness and discretion. Doubtless the unexpected arrival of a son to one aged MP was my doing. The event was touted as evidence of his vigor, and he received the largest majority in his next election.

This causes me to wonder. If much of England is related to royalty through the bastardy of kings, those early Fitz-whatevers, then how much does common blood bear royalty through dalliance of queens? A blasphemous thought, yet delicious nonetheless.

Under Freddie's advice, Algie acceded to opening the larger saloons and galleries to public view on Wednesday afternoon. Because I grew up on the estate, I became the tour guide. I was now a teacher with a new crop of students each week to instruct on wormy French furniture, imitation Kent wall décor, and copies of Van Dyck, though never mentioned as such. Through research in the family archives, I pieced together the history conveyed here earlier. Most tourists were Yanks, that country little affected by post-WWI inflation.

SLANDERLEY

Eventually we created a tea house tent where we served overpriced Lipton's to haul in even more of their money.

Then one day I met a winsome visitor who would change all our lives

An Unexpected Guest

One Wednesday afternoon the usual motley assortment of tourists included a young raven-haired, porcelain-complexioned beauty. While dressed in a flashy way, a too-bright cherry wool suit, clinging silk blouse with décolleté, and silver heels, she asked questions I'd have expected from an Oxbridge don. "Those cartouches remind me of Angelica Kauffman, though of course they are too bright." By the tour's end we neglected others as we continued what became a private conversation.

While the others filed out to their cars, she turned around and extended her hand. "Ravina Elmsby. You show such a fine knowledge of the estate one would think you the heir, Mr.--, sorry I forget your name."

"Quirk. But it is I who should complement you for your perspicacious questions. Most can't tell a Chippendale from a Georgian chair, if you can imagine that. Most think our tapestries are factory made." I rolled my eyes in dismay.

"What a trial this must be for you. I can tell you welcome questions of more depth."

"Not really a bother, except when the group is all American. When I hear their boisterous honks as they approach, I wish I could cancel the tour. They poke at portraits, try to open locked doors, finger silver candlesticks, lift plates to read the marks under plates, and want to know the price of everything. Some even ask to buy an item, as though the house were a big jumble sale."

She laughed lightly, like a buzzing bee. Her reassuring smile seemed familiar.

"Excuse my impertinence. Have we met before?"

"Not formally, though I visited the estate many years ago. I was orphaned at age twelve, my parents were distantly related to the local Elmsbys. They adopted me, so I came with my older sister Davina Elmsby to visit Letitia. Sloth let me play in the beach cottage and watched me wading to prevent me from drowning. What I'd give to be able to live down there! I love the thrumming waves and banging tide on the rocks." She flicked her hair toward the serpentine path.

"Ah, perhaps I have noticed you then. Yet you haven't been here for many years. I don't recall seeing you at Letitia's wedding events."

"No, after finishing school I went to London for art classes. I've been about the Continent sketching and painting. The Elmsbys have been most generous in treating me as their own. My adopted mother Ursula has been ailing, so I returned recently to comfort her. Learning of these tours, I thought it would be fun to see how the main rooms are being displayed."

"So your art training explains your close examination of the brush work on the portraits. I suspect you know I described several copies as genuine."

"Yes, and because I didn't embarrass you, I hope you will honor a special request. I'd like to see the painting of Charlotte de Loverly, the lady in white. I know it is in the private family apartments. I hesitate to pressure you."

"No, difficulty. You are almost a friend of the family, so I am pleased to assent."

I led her up the heavily carved staircase to the top landing, where the portrait held command over anyone approaching. As Ravina stood transfixed before the vision of Charlotte radiant in flowing white silk with puffed sleeves, hat in hand, I observed a similar coloring between the two women, green-eyed brunettes with wavy hair. She could have been a descendant of Lady Charlotte.

Ravina's whisper broke the spell. "Are there any other paintings of her? I'd like to see how age changed her beauty."

"Alas, no. She died a year after this painting was completed."

"How tragic! What was the reason? An illness? Of course—in those days it would have been childbirth."

"No, sadly she committed suicide for reasons unseemly. She arrived here unexpectedly one day, claiming to be the widow of second son Roderick de Loverly, who lived in Italy as a painter. The family was still in mourning for him and knew neither of her nor the cause of his death. She explained her husband died suddenly of an infection after cutting himself with a canvas knife.

"Naturally Lord Bruce welcomed her to stay in family apartments. Her sylvan tones and grace won all over. Bruce's mother encouraged him to propose, for he was getting long in the tooth in his delay to produce and heir. When Charlotte accepted, he ordered the portrait to honor their engagement. The artist, Henry Taglioni-Churchill, died soon afterward, so this is a rare sample of his work."

"She must have been quite pleased. It is the no doubt best portrait in the house."

"I suppose so. Yet Bruce was a poor deluded youth! He and the others overlooked how beauty masked questionable morality. She cheated at cards, and likely stole a guest's jewelry. A family friend, the paranoid Earl of Fflummer, was less enchanted. He urged Bruce patience and suggested a private investigator before setting a date. They located an Italian detective to verify Charlotte's story." I paused to whisk some dust off the frame.

"Please, end the suspense! What did the detective find?"

"Something happened before we obtained his report. One spring day she disappeared during the lilac fete. We found her body crushed on the rocks beneath the stone bridge in the copse. On her desk we found a letter to Bruce from the Italian detective. She had intercepted and opened it. It revealed how Roderick died of poison and Charlotte was wanted for murder. Not only that, she and Roderick were never married. Italian police believed her motive was his refusal to wed."

Ravina shook her head objecting. "Are you having a laugh on me? That is the sort of story one finds in the romantic magazines my maid reads."

"On my word of honor, it's completely true. We have the letter in our archives. Bruce was bereft, though eventually he came to his senses. He left in his will that Charlotte's portrait be hung here in perpetuity, a reminder to later family of Charlotte's malevolence. I can't say that it has done any good. He did marry a Baroness Danvers, but they were childless, so the line transferred to some inbred cousin, Lord Leo's line."

"I see his purpose," averred Ravina. "This vision of flawless physical being should not be mistaken with intelligence and moral standards. That combination is found only in heaven." Glancing at her fake diamond watch, she exclaimed, "I'm late for a very important date. I must rush off. By the way, what is your Christian name?"

"Edmund."

"Edmund? Eddie? I think I'll call you Quirkie." And off she dashed, heels tapping down the stairs.

I remained mesmerized by her heavy enveloping scent suffusing the air. It was floral, yet not exactly pleasant, a bit sharp to the nose. Her unexpected appearance so shook me that I took a long overdue fortnight's holiday.

I headed north to hike about Wales. I started by climbing Pen Y Fan, almost 3000 feet high in the Brecon Beacons. Then I ambled along Offas Dyke Path, overnighting along the way. My hope was to meet two ladies near Llangollen known for their fabulous library. They were ailing, yet happy to show me their luscious collection when I offered a small donation. From the medieval city of Chester I caught trains to speed back to Cornwall.

Arriving home, Algie informed of a return to the long-missed annual costume ball. Though she no longer lived at Slanderley, Letitia agreed to help organize this exclusive event. She demanded I assist in designing and ordering decorations, hiring temporary staff, and signing an orchestra. In comprising the guest list, I delighted to see Letitia included Ravina.

"Davina Elmsby is planning to safari in Africa, and already advised me she will be away then. She wrote her adopted sister has returned to the area. She was such a sweet girl, never intruding on our gossipy fun. I wonder what she looks like now that she is grown up. She was so scrawny and ill-kempt in her hygiene."

I didn't want to let on that I had already met Ravina, and she had outgrown all her youthful bad habits, as well as filled out like a dance hall girl. But I remained quiet. For the first time I'd encountered a woman I could desire as a mate. This bittersweet fate haunted my free moments. If only I could reveal the truth of my being a first born son, deserving of Slanderley. Only a miracle would do so. I buried my face in Letitia's charcoal-furred spaniel, a stand-in for Ravina's hair.

On the evening of the ball, the moon rose full and pregnant, a shimmering golden melon at the peak of sweetness. The air stirred with a medley of refreshing scents: lilac, damp moss, bark, azaleas, mint, old oak leaves, and calla lilies. Wisps of ground fog enhanced the guests' welcome with fancy.

As each nymph, knight, and sea captain entered, I sensed peace overtake me. Lusting for Ravina was useless. I could never possess her. All I could do was meet her requests whenever she happened to be on the estate. It might amount to little more than taking a cape, or opening a door, which I would do without a hint of my love. Suddenly I sensed an electric shock through my body.

"You look marvy tonight, Quirkie!"

I turned about to meet Ravina, splendid in an exact copy of Charlotte's white gown and hat, the most scintillating creature to grace Slanderley in a century. It was enough to make one believe in reincarnation.

Unseemly Coupling

Ravina attended the ball with Philip Elmsby, her cousin by adoption. Despite coming from a poorer branch of the line, he seldom lacked for money, and spent freely on his daily escapades. His love for fast machines drew Algie into his confidence. He was also a deft horseman with the sense to let Algie win any spontaneous races through the fields. Given his wheat blond hair and well-toned body, women gravitated toward his company. General opinion held Philip to be engaged in a mildly illegal or slightly forbidden activity, though no proof ever surfaced. Perhaps his doubters were too envious of his *joie de vivre*. That he was fabulously handsome assisted his well-known womanizing.

Ravina clearly thought him delightful. While dancing they moved as one, eyes only for each other, much laughter passing in between. Other men pushed in to partner her. Even Algie circled her about the room and cracked a grimace of gaiety. Aware of Algie's avoidance of small talk, Ravina kept up a steady monologue. He was guffawing in response to her buzz, and I wondered what she was speaking about.

Ravina became a regular visitor to Slanderley, accompanied by Philip or some other handsome suitor. Algie basked in their company and that of her high-spirited friends. The rooms resounded playful hoots during ducking for apples in flour or jousting with epées. New tennis court nets appeared, while the old ones were resurfaced. Even Algie brought out his old white flannels to play. I hadn't seen him so happy in years.

Algie's only restriction was that people not descend to the tempting beach with its old fishing cottage and boat. On his first childhood visit to the lagoon, he and his nanny came upon a shipwreck victim. The sight of that green, bloated body froze in his mind to be associated with the beach, forever after a place of horror.

My duties now more managerial, I hired an under butler, Kenneth, an Oxford economics student sent down for some nefarious acts not to be mentioned. He was in type my twin, as reclusive and bookish as I. It is he who had more daily contact with Ravina as he took over most of the meet-and-greet.

Were I to encounter Ravina, she would try to draw me in, but I played deaf. Which is not to say I didn't peek into a window to admire her latest attire and the form beneath. One day I turned the corner smack into her. She was in a tennis frock, her face sweaty.

"I've got you at last, Quirkie. Have I done anything to upset you?"

"Not at all, madam."

"Then why do you avoid me all the time, yet hide nearby to watch me? I say, that's very impolite and not what I'd have expected from you." She tapped her racquet on my chest.

I breathed in her floral perfume mixed with perspiration, a luscious aroma. "My apologies. I just felt—"

"It was inappropriate to chat with a guest? Please stop being so old-fashioned. It is the Twenties. We are moving forward!"

"Quite right. I'm sorry. As a staff leader I feel bound to stricter rules. It was nothing personal."

"From now on please," she leaned in and whispered, "at least smile and give a welcome. You surely can do that much for me."

Then she stepped aside and let me pass, smacking me on my derriere with the racquet. "Remember, Quirkie, be nice!"

Several weeks later Algie called me into his dressing room to announce, "Miss Elmsby and I are to be married at the end of May. She will be bringing a personal maid, as well as a long-time retainer, Mrs. Anvil, who will take over as housekeeper. Please prepare everyone accordingly."

"Excuse me, milord, but we have done very well with the Danderfull couple. If we let her go, he will follow."

"That is not my problem, Quirk. Ravina insists, and I agree with her. We can have only one head housekeeper."

I could scarcely see my way out, my rage darkening my vision. How could Ravina wed Algie? How could she introduce her own choice of servant almost equal to my authority? I was peeved personally and professionally, petulant on all particular points.

Nor could I understand Algie's decision. It wasn't a case of preferring men so much as avoiding an intimate connection with anyone. Nan had reminded him of his eventual duty, but that could come years from now, so long as the woman was of conceivable age. He advised Nan to be patient, that he understood his duty and would step in when ready. Apart from the ritual of a hunt, he was always happiest solely in the company of a dog or two. The thought of him in bed with Ravina left me discombobulated.

There remained my oath to Lord Leo, to protect Algie no matter what. Hence I displayed no resistance in arranging the wedding social events. Ravina wished a small ceremony in the manor chapel. It was unused since the arrival of the Protestant de Loverlys. Following days of cleaning and refurbishment the pews glowed with oil and beeswax candles stood on enormous candelabra. We placed a rug over a floor slab announcing the bones of St. Twewewekesbury (Toosbury), and chipped other unseemly Papist signs from the walls and altar.

In private I punched my pillows as I cursed the future. How hellish to face Ravina daily as Lady de Loverly. I always knew one day a wife would arrive, a dull, suitable heir bearer from a family no lower than an earl. Such a wife could not disrupt our lives as Ravina promised through her dramatic energy and modern ways. I was torn between my lust for Ravina and my disdain for her coopting the manor. The latter increased my sympathies for Algie, so unsuited for a commoner. Times had changed, though, and no one would interfere to prevent what was once an inappropriate conjunction.

Although staff were expected to attend the ritual and parties, I excused myself with a claim Aunt Jemima needed me in London. I did go to her to meet Mr. Titmouse. Given my unexpected arrival, they arranged a civil ceremony so I could give her away. Their obvious happiness distracted me from the nuptials in Cornwall.

By the time I returned, the newlyweds had left for Monte Carlo. Algie welcomed the warmth, while Ravina wished days at the gaming tables with her newfound wealth. Thus it was weeks before I met Ravina's selected staff.

First to arrive was Lisette, a typical lady's maid: haughty, seductive, and attired in Ravina's silken hand-me-downs. Kenneth was soon noticed traipsing off in the woods with her. She refused to eat luncheon in the servants' quarters, which suited me fine. In spite of her name, I guessed her to be from some town in the horrible North, for her speech was incomprehensible Yorkish.

The housekeeper, Mrs. Anvil, was a greater problem. Her black dress draped over a bony frame like a shroud. Contorting her face was a large scar across her left cheek, pulling her mouth up into a half-skull grin. Her skin was sallow and dry like parchment. She walked with a slight limp, an effort that made her breath rasp like a death rattle when ascending the stairs. The "Mrs" was an honorific applied to housekeepers, wed or not, and she clearly was not. At first glance my response was pity, until I met her eyes, hard black fiery coals with words of warning etched upon them.

"Mr. Quirk, I am not pleased with what I see here. Too lax. Too much chumminess. All staff levels eating together! Keys passed around as if they are everyone's right. I have requested of Mrs. Viscous separate meals sent to my sitting room. And I want *all* the keys for you can't trust the others."

"At your service, Mrs. Anvil. You may eat alone, as I do not mind the conversation of a scullery maid. But as for the keys, since you are the only stranger here, why should we trust you?"

My reply set the first skirmish in an unending battle. My main concern was to prevent staff from leaving. Daily I found myself soothing the nerves of one or another of her latest victims. Mrs. Anvil reintroduced Victorian practices long vanished. Even though no morning fires need be set, she had an alarm awaken staff before dawn. Once dressed, they gathered while she read from the Old Testament. She insisted upon caps and older style uniforms that looked well yet proved cumbersome during work. As maids went about their cleaning, she followed about like an anteater, picking at an invisible fly speck that required an entire window be rewashed. From now on tea breaks consisted of cooled pots left from upstairs along with stale breads and biscuits. Were it not for the decent wages and my interventions, everyone would have left.

The newlyweds returned, a chalk white Ravina and burnished bronze Algernon. A daily schedule soon brought order. Ravina spent each morning on the phone from her satin spread bed, plotting social affairs with all the efficiency of an aide-de-camp. Following lunch, she consulted with decorators, dressmakers, milliners, shoemakers, and jewelers. When the fashion season arrived, she fled with Lisette to Paris for a weekend to choose evening gowns and be fitted. Instead she returned with some dresses called "garcons," boyishly cut, by a now-lauded designer named Coco. They were uncomplimentary to her curvaceous figure.

Ravina cheered us all by insisting Nan be brought back from her imprisonment in Chilsworth, with her personal maid Rose in an adjoining chamber. When she heard Algie comment in passing about Nan, his Aunt Euphoria, she grew red. "Really, Algernon, we are no longer in the middle ages. We don't send female family members to the nunneries or mad houses. I insist your aunt return to live here."

Nan joined her for tea, I in the background, to hear tales from Cornwall history. There was the family of astronomer Daniel Gumb, who lived in the Cheesewring cave he carved with his bare hands. Less believable was her account of Sir Veredibix sacrificing virgins on Bodmin Moor, his notion of an ancient Celtic ritual.

Nan recounted her own past pixilated behaviors. She had distributed pamphlets in support of Oscar Wilde during the time of his trial. Hearing of Isadora Duncan, she donned sheer togas over her naked body and danced over church lawns. She arranged for her blouse to slide too far just as she handed a duke a tea cup. "No single man was ever enough for me. In the process I acquired quite a good array of jewelry. All mine, not part of the de Loverly horde."

Nan also helped Ravina appreciate Algie's upbringing. Over tea once Ravina commented how Algie lacked affection, even in private. Nan responded, "It's those public boys' schools that ruin them. All those beatings and faggings turn many into scaredy cats. That's how we can ensnare them and get our way. So look at the bright side, Ravina. Think of those latest emeralds he gave you. They are a perfect match for your eyes."

Despite their age differences, Nan and Ravina shared equal exuberance. Nan ordered one of the new record players for her sitting room. There the two played the latest jazzy band music while practicing the Heebie-Jeebies and Job Rot. Lacking good partners nearby, they even went to the Embassy night club in London. Ravina also took Nan to Paris and they returned with streamlined dresses, some with Art Deco designs. They kept the chauffeur busy with day trips to places with what they called "smart people."

Ravina's rare faults made curious demands on service. One was her preference in flowers, azaleas. Soon the gardeners tore out shaded shrubbery to fill in with those malodorous blooms. Her azalea perfume was custom made by a London perfumist. . I agreed with the judgement of Widgeon, "Smell like the scum of a fish pond to me, it do." Oh for a gardenia, just one!

Then there was the laundry. Ravina's decorator Barnaby had once lived with a Gurdjieff-type sect, during which he became convinced that happiness in life required sleeping on sheets of a particular color on a particular day. He created the Mystical Cycle of Hues, twenty-four shades, which mixed and matched in a most bewildering fashion. Ravina believed the system had roots in Druid and Egyptian ritual, proof enough to her artistic ear of its healthful influence. (She ignored that few ancient Egyptians lived beyond twenty-five.) She brought twenty-four sets of linens and pyjamas, leaving laundry women to curse, for there was no way they could cheat on the daily change. "Argh, it's cerise again? Hate that color 'cause it runs."

And so it was that life for Slanderleyans stumbled along.

A Dull Interlude

Oh, the days and weeks that followed. The particular shape of the couple's relationship puzzled. Similar to aristocratic practice, they slept separately, their apartments connected by a small private chamber between dressing rooms. Just when, how, or whether they had sexual congress was a topic of downstairs chatter. The bed strippers remained mum, perhaps in exchange for a favorable bonus to their pay.

Algie continued to spend inclement days in his Trophy Room, a book in his lap, the same one at the same page for hours. On fine days he went into the woods to return with an ankle decorated by a rabbit snare, or the feathers of a wood pigeon shot for its interminable "TAKE two cows, TAFfy" call. Where his friends enjoyed the benefits of living along the coast, he understandably resisted boating. He was, as might be concluded, and easy ruler to please so long as one left him alone when he wished.

Though they breakfasted separately, the two met during tea and other meals. To my surprise, Ravina was the most attentive of wives, dipping a napkin in a finger bowl to swipe at a tiny smear of food on his collar or dropping the precise amount of sugar for his cup. He returned brief, gentle smiles in thanks. He glowed when he noticed her in the garden clipping lilac sprays.

So he surprised me one afternoon when I was pouring sherry in the trophy room, Algie bolted upright in his chair as though suddenly awoken.

"Damned slut."

"Excuse me, milord?

"Women are an abomination. St. Paul was right. Impure. Defiling!"

"Ahem, all women, sir?

"Insufferable teases and liars. Vile. Disgusting. Be glad you're single, Quirk."

Nonetheless, Algie neither disparaged Ravina directly, nor mistreated her to my knowledge. Only later did I think he could have been thinking of other women, such as those now blasted on city society pages.

Indeed, I soon found each more complicated than I long assumed. Algie welcomed the increase in activities Ravina devised. She reinstituted the annual costume ball, and invited the local church to use the grounds for its fetes. Now in addition to Slanderley's place on the hunt season schedule, she introduced long weekends for nearby aristocracy and fortnights for those contacts living in or about London.

With Aunt Jemima gone, and Freddie handling major business affairs, no one filled as estate secretary. Still I was surprised when Ravina called me in one day and asked me to assist in her social invitations and calendar. Oh, to be near her regularly was a challenge to my confused emotions. I compensated by visiting Rose more often for evening snogs.

"The azaleas and will be in bloom in a month, so I want a lavish party to applaud them. I'll advise the women to wear evening dresses in the glorious shades from pink to carmine. I've advised Mrs. Viscous to a Sunday picnic of foods all of similar shades: apples, peaches, steak tartare, beet, and such, all sprinkled with paprika. We can set the date to the next bank holiday to make it easier for several of those working folks I wish to invite." She fluttered about like a light-drawn moth while exclaiming.

"I'm changing some décor in several guest rooms temporarily to be more in keeping with the floral theme. Gherkin will become Fern, rather easy since both are green, and Pintail will need more changes to become Hen's Bane."

"Yes, milady. If you provide color charts, I will see whether the local upholsterer can provide."

"No need, Quirkie. My friend Barnaby in London is seeing to new drapes, pillows, and pictures accordingly. He already has a suitable supply of many provisions from his samples."

She next handed me a sheet written in green ink on foolscap. Her handwriting was scrolled and childish, the result of early poor schooling prior to her adoption, I guessed.

"Now as to this guest list, I've already checked that the actress Maud Culm's play will have closed. She is looking forward to resting here. I must warn you though to avoid being alone with her. As you know, I am fond of stage people, but she is beyond the bend in some ways. She almost brought down the last Bishop of Canterbury with her shenanigans."

"I'll see that only female staff concern her needs. What about this Max Mallobar? Has he been here before?"

"No, he's an archeologist, digs among the Arabs. I knew Algie would enjoy his company. His wife is a mystery writer, so watch out for her snooping. I daresay she is worse than you."

"Milady?" I stepped back in feigned horror.

"Come now, I know how you wear those soft-soled shoes to creep about like a little boy hoping to catch his parents doing something bad. The same for your phone snoops. It's why I trust you, because you already know everything."

The Azalea Extravaganza, her first big event, proved a fabulous success. Algie took the archeologist out to spots on the estate suspected of ancient habitation. Several times I caught the skulking mystery wife where she didn't belong. However, her excellent Devon upbringing led her to be gracious toward some of the clumsier visitors. As for Maud Culm, well, less is more. From this first attempt, I recognized the creativity and eccentricity central to Ravina's relation to the world. Later fetes, balls, and excuses for celebration only ramped up the unique presentation. One time she managed to have a zoo bring some Mhorr Gazettes and Addaxes to a pasture, her "Off to Africa Plains" weekend. (After a Zebra broke into a stable for an interspecies encounter, Algie plugged any repeat.)

Knowing she lived in poverty until adolescence, I understood her outsized plans as making up for what she never had. Her Elmsby adoptive parents were very old money, given to rotting silk drapes, dog-chewed chintz, and a rocky croquet lawn. They saw to her being prudently dressed and sent to a ladies finishing school, but being Methodist, they were fearful of fun. Perhaps they are why she gravitated toward her impulsive cousin Philip.

Ravina equally enjoyed dinner parties, though these served a purpose beyond conviviality. Having been poor she expended wealth toward relief and prodded others to do likewise. At one dinner I overheard her encourage the principal of a school for the feebleminded, which needed playground equipment, be matched with the president of the bridge club, who created a charity tournament. She even trapped the odious Bishop's wife into joining her in distributing Easter baskets at a home for wayward girls.

Ravina's third cause was her art. In time she gained Algie's approval to head to London for lessons, gallery openings, and plays. She called him daily to report on her activities. She needn't have because he readily fell into his own interests, while pining for her. He passed day after day in the Trophy Room with orders for trays to be left at the door. Later he even took to evenings out alone, "a man needs to be with just other men," he explained.

In time Algie even allowed Ravina to renovate the fishing cottage into an art studio. Now she returned to her first love, sketching and painting, and even spent nights asleep below.

She went down with a hamper of food, insisting she wanted no servants disadvantaged by the steep and treacherous hike to see to her needs. She created a basket and pulley system to send laundry or other goods up and down.

She befriended local fishermen, who advised her in the purchase and handling of her own boat. She was a good swimmer, yet cautious and knowledgeable about the treacherous tides and sudden storms. The attraction of sketching land from sea was great, however. Fortunately the lagoon was often ruled by slight zephyrs and she found many interesting spots from within for her drawing.

So like all of us, Ravina was a knitting ball of ravels, if to great extreme. Algie, on the other hand, seemed more monotonous, yet that changed as he warmed up to visitors and their addition of variety to conversation. The more guests, the less he need say. His dancing improved, and he discovered how easy it was to please wives of two-left-footed men without having to say anything. By age thirty he appeared very much the appropriate Lord of the Manor, one Lord Leo would approve.

With maturity came a new interest in the business matters of the estate. The world was getting troublesome, hints of war trumpets yet again in Germany. That country's economic collapse, matched by one in the United States, left the inheritance class bewildered. Some great houses came down in dynamite to sell land to speculators and developers. Managed by Freddie, Slanderley escaped the threats. He was a veritable wizard, slick as Mercury in his dealings.

Now Ravina's major assistant, I depended upon Freddie for information. He surprised me with his newfound praise. "I tell you, Eddie, Algie is developing a sophisticated understanding of finance and investment. It is not just my decisions that are responsible for the unexpected wealth. Algie says he gets advice from other men. I don't know who they are, but they know a lot more than advisors in the city about Continental industry."

One brief, sad note disrupted the predictable boredom. This was a weekend for the many artists Ravina befriended during her visits to London. By then she was redoing some of Slanderley's rooms in Art Deco. The Dungeon walls were whitewashed and new lighting added to serve as a sculpture gallery of elongated dancers and sinewy panthers.

Among the guests was her decorator friend Barnaby. He arrived in a forest green Riley Mark III roadster. As Barnaby roared in, Ravina rushed Algie over to introduce the two men. Algie shook hands but focused his eyes upon the gleaming automobile.

"How do you find driving with the gear box moved from the right to the center? Was it hard to adjust?" Algie asked.

"Not for me. In fact I enjoy having my right hand free to smoke. The brakes handle better than the previous model as well."

"I suppose that is helpful given the potential speed. Can you really take it to 60 miles an hour? Not that one ever uses that option. Certainly it wouldn't be practical on the single lanes around here."

"Right. And the rear wheel drive is a bit tricky sometimes. But think about knowing you have all that potential when you need it for a quick pass on a highway."

Ravina surprised me by adding, "And it gets forty miles to the gallon of petrol." Where did she get this information?

Algie ran his hand lovingly over the bonnet. "How about you taking me for a spin after lunch tomorrow? And join me as a guest at the next Grand Prix in Monaco? I hear it is the most dangerous new course. D'you know the first winner's car was painted this color?"

"Yes, I ordered it specially. What a fine invitation! Of course I will take you out and accept your Monaco offer."

Ravina, standing by this discussion, planted a hug and sisterly kiss on Barnaby. Then she grabbed Algie's hand, "How nice that the two of you can will get along. Am I invited?"

"I think this best a men's only trip, my dear. But I promise to take you to Monaco next year. Now, Barnaby, you must sit by me during meals. I see we have much in common."

The next afternoon was rain free, so the men took off after lunch while others played tennis, rode, or sunned at the beach. By cocktail time the men had not returned, and the guests whispered in worry and requested additional fills to allay their fears. Ravina sent word for dinner to be held back.

At almost eight o'clock, Kenneth brought two constables into the room. "Very sad news," said one after introductions. "There has been an accident. His Lordship is being treated for minor bruises, and will soon return, but Mr. Bumsted was killed on impact."

Ravina fainted, so I carried her to a lounge and called for brandy. She revived quickly, whispering Barnaby's name.

"Please tell us all the details," she demanded of the police.

"They were on a back road by Tickle Moor when Mr. Bumsted missed a curve. He overcorrected and crashed into a stone wall. He flew over the bonnet head first. His Lordship was cradling him at the side of the road. He had done what he could but death was instantaneous. Lord Algernon was quite bereft so we had him taken on to the surgery for a sedative."

"But Barnaby was such a good driver," cried Ravina. "I don't understand."

"Yes, milady, but we understand it was a new car with extra horse power. The road was new to him as well, and you know how those sharp curves can jump in on the lanes."

I intervened. "Please, milady, do rest while I see to dinner served for the guests." I knew it was too late for them to depart, that many would take off before breakfast.

Instead, Ravina stood and planted her hand outward. "No, I must see to everyone's care as hostess. Send word down that we shall dine in ten minutes."

Others gathered round her, hens protecting a chick, while those close to Barnaby formed a second circle of mourners. Algernon ordered the black drapes of grief brought down and hung on the windows. The next day Ravina and her friends left for London to see to Barnaby's funeral. She remained there several weeks, and returned subdued yet ready to move forward.

Algie met her at the door to wrap his arms around, a rare expression of affection. In the weeks following, he searched her out for walks about the garden. He acceded to her request for a half year's full mourning, which meant cancelling the next costume ball and his dropping Slanderley from the hunt schedule.

Clarice Stasz

Until Death

When time for the next costume ball approached, Ravina chose the Mystic Circle of Colors to be its theme. Once again she temporarily renamed guest rooms. Gherkin was Green of course, while Pumpernickel for some unexplained reason became Daffodil. At least none became Puce.

Rather than hire a jazz band, she had me search for a Hungarian gypsy orchestra. "Barnaby said the tremolo of the cimbalom and wild violin cadenzas sent him into ecstasy. Imagine all the shades of the rainbow spinning wildly like Sufis during their playing!" That meant, alas, only male musicians who, apart from the conductor, spoke gibberish.

On the other hand, the three a.m. buffet consisted of tortes and pastries sufficient to send everyone into sugar shock, if not keel over from a fatty heart attack. It was the best spread ever at a ball. A Hungarian restaurant from London provided the savory stews and wild fowl. Bakers flew in from their shop Rádi Pékség in Eger, much to Mrs. Viscous's dismay. She complained for weeks afterward about all the powdered sugar and goose fat infecting her cooking pans.

Ravina wore a Hungarian folk dress of silk and heavily bejeweled red velvet vest. Algernon even broke his tradition by placing a fuchsia point in his jacket pocket. The Czardas alternation of slow dance with raucous spinning left several with ankle sprains and one left with a broken wrist. I saw to the individual comfort of a young woman in harem dress who slid on some spilt champagne.

Before that charitable deed, however, I went into the library for a few minutes of quiet. I couldn't enter, however, because beside the hearth stood Ravina, her arms around a masked monk. Deep in whispered conversation, they were there to hide, but what? I stepped back in wonder. I hadn't recalled a monk in the crowd, nor did I see one afterward. The scene left me unsettled for several days.

Weeks later Letty called me up. "Ravina has released you to assist me with the Hunt Ball. You were such a marvy help with the Hungarian delight."

Widgeon drove me over to Pursesnatch, the Horsham manor, where I was led into the morning room. Letty sat chewing the nib of her pen. "I regret I brought you here under false pretenses. I don't really need your assistance on the ball."

I backed away. "Now, milady. Please, not again."

"No, no—it has nothing to do with me. I'm here concerning Ravina. Please take a seat."

I chose the farthest one across the room.

"Has it not seemed strange there is yet an heir, let alone a spare? She has had enough time for both with a long space in between."

"I admit we have wondered such in the servant lounge. She is very healthy, and Algie as well."

"Excuse me for my candor, but they have done the necessary. She has been very distraught for several years and has recently considered their adopting a distant relation or two."

"Ah, that explains her interest in family history. I had to invite some unacquainted relations to the ball. One slipped on champagne and I had to soothe her, a most winsome young lady." This realization had me think secretly of the monk, along with the couple's recent shows of affection.

Letty leaned forward. "I tell you this so you won't be surprised. First she must raise the possibility with Algernon. She confided in me to add encouragement. Although it is an unusual choice, it is hardly rare."

I reflected on bachelor aristocrats who adopted wards, who might lack any blood relation. "Yes, I see, milady. I can think of several novels to place in the Trophy Room for Algie's leisure reading. *Duke Dungballs Dilemma* and such."

"They haven't given up, but Ravina knows Algie wants to keep control of the situation, as she knows Lord Leo would wish."

After further chatter I left with assurances I would keep this conversation confidential. When I returned to Ravina at her desk, she gave a wink. "I am considering some changes for a permanent guest or two. Do look at the Thistle apartments and let me know what conveniences need to be added."

Thus passed the months. Ravina brought forth no male heir. Mrs. Anvil became ever more devious and skulky in her attempts to harass service. Similar to Don Juan, I expanded my list of women I pleasured. In contradiction to those around us, who had to sell off land, furniture, manuscripts, and paintings to Americans, Slanderley's wealth grew under Freddie's financial wizardry. His own holdings expanded proportionately, yet he did not retire. While Freddie and I were facing down middle age, our youthful desires and thoughts had not been sanded down by experience. We lacked maturity to appreciate the peace must end. Slanderley must change, for nothing stays the same. In Barnaby's memory, his followers added four more hues to the Mystical Cycle, further complicating the linen conundrum. The azaleas emblazoned a spectacular season.

Following more than a decade's absence, Philip's car was observed parked on a back forested lane. Sloth reported he eyed Philip approaching the beach cottage when Ravina was also there. If Algie received word of such encounters, he never signaled.

One day I entered the morning room to face Ravina, face in her arms on the table, sobbing silently.

"Is anything wrong, milady?"

"Oh, Quirkie, I can't stand this any longer. You are the only one I trust here. I need your help, as a friend. I'm in great trouble and need your reassurance. Don't interrupt. Please listen in full, else I lose my courage. Afterward, please leave without a question or comment."

I stood puzzled and silent.

"I know you once desired me, that my marriage to Algernon aroused jealousy. You've wondered if I wanted only his position and wealth. I did, though not until after the wedding. I married him because I was forced to."

She took out a monogrammed handkerchief and began to cry.

"One evening Philip and I attended a dinner at Letitia's. Algie rushed out of the men's smoking sanctuary to say Philip received an emergency call to return home immediately. He asked Algernon to drive me home to my parents as a favor. Then he rejoined the men, and did not speak with me until time to depart.

"He drove as if overtaken by a demon, headed on a fork away from my home, and parked in a dark copse. There he forced himself on me in the most unspeakable and perverse manner, said I now had to marry him, first, because otherwise he'd blast my name as a slut all over and second, because he'd learned Philip was in some kind of serious legal trouble and could ruin him. Knowing I would protect Philip from any blackmail, I consented. I cared not about my own reputation.

I moved in closer, but she held out her palms to stop me.

"Don't think I was totally a victim. Algernon was the wealthiest bachelor around. Having known poverty before adoption, I wanted insurance of continued comfort. Algie followed through by underwriting Philip's emigration to Australia. Only after Philip departed did I discover Algie had lied about the party emergency. Rather, he informed Philip I had already left with someone else. So we each were tricked and kept apart.

"I know it was wrong to wed falsely, but I absorbed my stepparents' philosophy of charity. I naively convinced myself I was doing this to be a Robin Hood, use my new wealth to help the needy. I can't say I was always successful, for I certainly spent a lot of Algernon's riches on myself."

"You deserved them, for look at what you had to endure."

"I suppose there is some truth there. Algernon believes I make love to every man who comes to the house. He has become more demented that way since the accident."

"Yet you seem closer now."

"True, he has shown an unexpected kindness. Without intending he has forced my understanding of him. I think of his troubled childhood, his emotional constrictions. Did not my own hard youth drive my immoral choices? I considered our early years, how he did try to adapt to my wishes. That was his form of love, not physical gentleness. How could he have been any different?"

Her voice cracked in emotion. She wiped her blotchy face with a napkin. She transformed into a fully-formed woman, her book of foolishness closed, and a focused life ahead.

"Perhaps my request will seem less strange in light of what I have confessed. If anything happens to me, no matter how nor when, whether tomorrow or in thirty years, swear you will protect Algernon. Keep him on his strict schedule and habits. He will never marry again, that I know. With fate on our side, an heir and perhaps spare will add to his happiness.

"However unfeeling his early years with me, Algernon opened the door to a life I could never have. I was smug, vain.

Marriage to Philip would have destroyed us both. He enjoys his new life in Australia. His recent return is at my request, and will be brief. I need his help on a different matter. Now give me your assurance by leaving without a word."

I stared a moment into her luminous viridescent eyes, turned, and padded away, distraught. She allowed me the most intimate confidence. I fell in love all over again, with the mature Ravina, not the flirty dramatic child.

After luncheon that day, Ravina left for London. When she returned the next evening. I was at a Slyme Gurney pub, the Middle Finger, and did not see her. Earlier that night Algie requested I lock him in the bedroom for he wished to retire early without any later interruption. He often did so to feel secure, despite my warning it was dangerous in case of fire. I checked the door at midnight to hear him snoring away.

The next morning Ravina was not in the morning room. Her maid advised me she likely slept in the cottage, that her bed had not been slept in. I sent Kenneth down to see if all was well. He reported back the rooms were empty but her boat was gone. We assumed she was out on the water.

By dusk, I went down myself and again found neither Ravina nor her craft. I suspected she remained on the water, too busy drawing to notice fading light. I returned to the manor, expecting her to call from the cottage that evening. None came. A most hysterical Algie set private detectives on the case, with no clues found to her absence. A day later he filed a report with the local constable. Despite their inquiries, the police too had no results.

SLANDERLEY

The house fell into virtual mourning. Inconsolable herself, Nan stepped in to sooth the rest of us. Daily Algie went to the beach, the place he always resisted, to watch the incoming tides. He ordered me stay on the phone in case she appeared at another port, perhaps thrown off course. Some evenings he went out, who knows where. Others he had the Bishop and his wife in for dinner, for he found the hackneyed tones of hope reassuring. So restless, he lost interest in his usual activities.

Then two months later a call from a constable solved the mystery. A woman's body had washed up on a beach several miles away. Though thrashing waves stripped away its clothing and jewelry, the police were certain. Algernon and Freddie went to perform the dreaded identification.

As soon as Algie walked past me upon his return, I could tell. He need not say, "Ravina."

A Surprise Missive

Funny to think that the course of my existence hung like a marionette from Algernon. With Ravina missing, I was back under his direction.

He depended upon me to arrange her burial in the family plot. We set the rite at midday so her city friends could come and leave on the same day. (Algernon arranged a special train to and from Exeter to speed their travel.) It was a surprisingly bright day, so the mourners' habits glowed like onyx. Azaleas cloaked her coffin. Before placing it in the crypt, Algie collapsed on top in great sobs. I had never seen him cry so since childhood.

The Bishop led him away, and we followed into the manor for a vast luncheon spread created by Mrs. Viscous. The buffet tables featured food from Ravina's childhood: pasties, squab pie, and cheeses to be followed by fudges, berry pies, and Saffron cake. Algie chose the menu, asserting that these nursery foods for many would be heartwarming. I was impressed by his consideration.

Mrs. Anvil brought out all the Mystic Circle linens and draped them on the furniture so the place was a veritable rainbow. To my surprise she had skipped the service, claiming she was needed in the house to prepare. She wore silken robes recalling Joseph's coat of many colors, and kept a slight smile on her face, one difficult to interpret.

When all departed in a rush to the train, Algie waved them off. Turning to me, he lightly clapped his hands. "Well, that's over. Now let's see the house is returned to its normal state. I want all those ugly sheets removed and destroyed."

Addressing Mrs. Anvil he advised, "And thank Mrs. Viscous for the delicious food. That is what I would like served again, no more of that 'grate-in dawph and noise' or that inedible 'reetattooee.' For breakfast, tell her I want more genuine figgy 'obbin, not those sugary Continental monstrosities."

I daresay all of us who ate at the manor were pleased by the change to the traditional Cornwall cuisine. Even the Bishop and his picky wife.

Ah, annoying though it is for you, dear reader, we must skip ahead some months to the day Algie brought grief to me and to others. We'd had a treacherous winter, the sea feeding on the storms' furies to siege the coastline as though to remind us that Nature, not we, ruled the land. Fog hung about, a guest outwearing his welcome. The croci cowered in their beds, while the nearby cobblestones shivered.

Algie appeared for breakfast that day no longer in mourning clothes. Only a black band covered his left sleeve.

"I must go away," he said, "to warmth and cheer. I can no longer stand this tomblike home. I want it totally shut up, the staff reduced to a minimum, and you must move with Nan to Chilsworth. Mrs. Viscous deserves a break and can stay with family—she's already been informed. Kenneth is staying in the beach cottage to keep watch on the sea. I expect several months away at least, so enjoy your freedom."

When I started to object, he banged his cane on the dog asleep at his feet. "No objections! I have allowed you to rule behind the scenes for years. I have decided and you must obey. I bear no argument! Now leave and see to these plans. I head to Monte Carlo on Thursday. Alone! It is my final break with Ravina, revisiting our honeymoon oasis."

What could I do? I belonged as much to Slanderley as Algie. Truth be told, I needed an escape as well. I could have no better release, for the weather was too rough for my usual walking tours. Freddie took the break to stay in London, so I couldn't just move in with him.

Little could improve upon Chilsworth for a respite. In addition to its own cook and maids, it provided central heating and all the modern conveniences. Having almost no chores, I enjoyed its well-appointed library to read and reflect. A long inclement season was time to travel in the mind under the guidance of Woolf, Wells, and Blyton. On less blustery days I could walk about with no sight of the villainous sea, still a reminder of Ravina. I even tried my hand at writing, and kept notes on my history at Slanderley, which have proved so useful in constructing this story.

Chilsworth's furnishings consisted of overflow from the estate, and reminded me of my happy days as a boy. Sometimes I went with my mother to Chilsworth to prepare it for longstanding visitors. She let me rummage about the attic, full of ancient toys and ministerial garb. I set up an old table into an altar, donned a robe, and gave accounts of fairies, goblins, and angels in heaven. Chilsworth was a much better play house than the beach cottage, though I seldom could visit it.

Nan tried to enjoy this small and damp-ridden exile. Though arthritic and losing her sight, she was more invigorating and amusing than those half her age. While never small-minded, she remained an uncanny judge of character. I tittered inwardly when she hoisted people on their own petards in a manner that would leave them drowned in compliments. To a porcine visitor she might reflect, "You are looking so *healthy* and *full of nutrition*, enough to share with others." To the opposite, she might intone, "That silk dress drapes on you like a hanger." Few listeners caught her irony.

In the mornings I read the news aloud while she ate. She was most interested in goings-on outside England. I read about the veteran uprisings in the United States, the election of a wealthy New Yorker of Dutch extraction, and the assassination of the French President. Such stories lifted her spirits. "Oh, how blessed to live in Cornwall. No one wants to come here, so we lack revolutions and war. Long may we stay weird?"

After a month we received a note from Algie. Rose read it aloud to us because she best interpreted his childish scrawls:

Dear Auntie,

Beaching etc. Casinos backarat.

I am now brown as a wog. People think I am from one of the coloniel countrys. Until I speak. Then they bow to give me due. I get free dinners in apologees.

Meeting agreeable sorts too. Stay away from French.
Have no return date.
Renting roadsters. Winding lanes in the mounteins.
Yrs,
A

"Typical Algie," we agreed. "Bad spelling and all." He seemed in splendid spirits taking advantage of people as well as the notable driving challenges. I couldn't help thinking about Barnaby there with him, what joy they'd share.

On dull afternoons Nan started her record player. No longer up to quick steps, she had me partner her in waltzes and slow polkas or czardas. She had learned enough Braille to play cards, but I think she read them as well because she was a cheat. She had to have seen bits of my hand. She was also a gambler, so I lost many quid to her.

Eventually the weather drew back, the squalls turned to showers. When dry, I went about and cleared areas where ancient bulbs hinted of a visit. Songbird activity promised an early spring as well. That had me hoping for sight of a rare wryneck.

Yes, I am wandering, so back to the day in question. I was in the library, my own black spaniel Boudicca warming my feet, with Volume Two of Havelock Ellis's *Studies in the Psychology of Sex* leading me into new territory of imagination. Rose swung open the door, waving an envelope in her hand.

"Sorry to butt in. There's another letter from Algie. I'll open and read to Nan once she's finished her tea. The stamp shows it's from Italy? What do you suppose he's doing there?

"Well, for certain he's not gone to admire the Sistine Chapel. You know how he hates both Italians and Catholics, considers them heathens and peasants."

"That's not all—he's in Venice! Look at the hotel address, the Danieli."

I was stunned. That 14th century palazzo is one of the most luxurious in Europe. Algernon enjoyed his comforts, but not those so overly-grand. I rather imagined him in an exclusive pension with very few guests.

"This is even curiouser. What drew him from the baccarat tables to the canals? Thank you for advising me, Rose. I'll be down shortly to hear your reading."

Before departing she bent down to leave a brief kiss, but the light scent of her lavender water roused my longing, and before she could pull away I wrapped my arms around her sinewy body, drew her into my lap, and melted my lips into hers.

She demurred. "After tea, Eddie. We must not upset Nan."

I smiled and let her go. Soon after my arrival Nan called us into the conservatory to admonish, "I know you two are, whatever they call it. I just wish you'd have the decency to wait until after elevenses when I nap. Your sighs and whoops are bittersweet to this crippled little body. If you only knew." Her eyes shifted to the left, adrift in reverie of her unwed, hardly virginal past.

"Sorry! Don't think I want you to stop altogether. It makes me feel less like being in nursing home where I'd overhear the gent next door handle his specials."

So we set off to the drawing room for tea and discovery. Nan had softened what could have been a rigid, formal atmosphere by replacing it with floral silks, chinoiserie, and interesting Japanese prints that depicted monks spying on maidens at bath. Given her scarlet kimono and liverish skin, she appeared this morning a proper Shogun's consort.

I grasped her hand. "I see a break in the weather coming. I think tomorrow you'll be able to sit in the conservatory in the afternoon and warm in the sun."

"Mr. Barnthistle says the kittiwakes are dropping off their cliffs in a mass suicide protest of the cold. He sent his best birder after them, thinking they'd make a good meal, but the poor hound drowned. Its memorial service is at two tomorrow afternoon, so I won't be sitting on the terrace. I've the loveliest new black crepe purchased during that trip to Chester. Pretty little sparkly things on the collar and cuffs I could almost see. You don't think that's too showy for mourning?"

"No, my lady. I expect the widowed bitch will find you in the best of taste. Just don't let the sun shine on the trim."

"Speaking of sun, let's have that letter from Algie. Can you imagine him in Venice? I see him on the Grand Canal in tweeds and shot gun trying to take down the gulls."

Rose tore open the envelope to pull out a sheet of onion skin decorated with the Danieli shield. Straightening herself taut, she read in a wry imitation of his raspy tenor:

Dearst Aunt de L,

Am in Italy, a rather loathesomenest corner of the globe. The people are greasy and fat, or greasy and emaciated. They speak gibberish and wiggle their hands while talking, to catch flies I presume. They do not bathe, which makes any close contact abhorrantly.

The order for visitors here is to drive from one set of ruins to another, bangle up ones feet with miles of walking about stoney churches and art galleries. Can see no use in statues of forein gods in various stages of undress, nor of that maudelin lady the Papists so blindly worship.

Bugs and heat. No shooting allowed.

After two days trial I quit the above meaningless tourism. My charming companion shares my preferences for fast drives about the countryside and liesurely meals at night, in rooms without Eyetalians of course. Ankchious to be home and hunt.

Accident didn't damage the car. Just a few sheep. Nasty incident there with stinking peasant. Paid enough for two flocks.

Will return May 4 unless other word follows.

Yours,

Algernon de L. [Immense scrawl]

"Well, it sounds as though the sea gulls are safe after all," quipped Nan, "but pity the poor sheep. What's the world coming to, people exceeding the thirty-mile speed mile limit?"

"Who is his companion?" wondered Rose. Who would travel about Italy with him? Perhaps he met up with one of his boring hunt friends. He doesn't say anything in explanation."

"Hold on," I interrupted. Isn't there some other note on the back?

"Oh, yes, you're right. Here it is. 'My companion is my new wife. Quirk to return to Slanderley at once to oversee all preparations. Nan to stay in Chilsworth' "

Nan began clawing the air in distress. "What's this? Eddie leaving? No! I don't want you to go! Who will make my currant brandy now? I won't be able to sleep at night without your company. Algie was cruel to force me here. This is too much to bear."

Rose thrust her arms around Nan to calm her. "Go Eddie, please. Leave this to me. I'll give her a nip of valerian tea."

I was grateful to depart, for upon seeing Nan's face furrowed with tears, I felt the same arise upon my own. I fled to pack my luggage and return to Slanderley.

Murder Most Nasty

So now I return to Slanderley, crypt of hapless memories. To serve Algernon again, with new wife, left me so desolate that the sight of the towers above the woodlands left me dizzy with anxiety.

I paused at Slanderley's private burial ground, where for the first time I knelt to respect that dear woman from my past. The cover slab read:

Ravina de Loverly
Beloved Wife
Never a Mother

That is all that marked her, not even dates. I wondered at the irony of her being identified by her conjugal tie. Head bowed, I requested her forgiveness in breaking my oath, in allowing Algie to leave. I asked God's guidance in facing the terrible task ahead.

Still distraught, I turned back to Slyme Gurney, where Aunt Jemima now lived there with a new husband Mr. Poots. She was widowed when Mr. Titmouse scattered rat poison in his garden shed and licked his fingers afterward. Upon entering her flat above Mr. Poots's butcher shop, she caught my mood.

"Eddie, my boy, we've missed you. You've lost more hair. Most becoming. I hope you weren't too lonely at Chilsworth. You must be pleased to be returning home."

"Oh, Auntie, I'm never lonely with Nan."

"Or Rose," she added with a wink.

Ignoring the tease, I explained, "To tell the truth I hesitate going back. I never imagined such a day could come to pass, but there remain the reminders of rapturous Ravina."

"Lord bless her soul! I never did understand her death. She was too fine a skipper of that boat to get into an accident. And bigger craft too. Remember when she played a trick on guests by hiring a ferry to take them to Aborigine Island, where actors faked ten murders there? The captain grew so hysterical that she took over the wheel to steer the party back through choppy seas. Don't make many like her much."

"No, Auntie, only in novels. Yet I agree with you that her death was suspicious. Have you any clue why it was other than accidental?"

"I do. Don't look so surprised. I happened to hear Philip Elmsby pass by here late the night of her disappearance. His noisy motor woke me up, close to ten thirty it was. And he got me again on his way out. My chimes struck midnight just as he passed."

"That's not surprising. Ravina mentioned to me that Philip arrived from Australia to help her with a special request only he could manage."

"Yes, but did Philip know you knew? He'd been sneaking about even when Ravina was away. I'd seen his yellow car in daylight, which is how I recognized the motor at night. Did she say how he was helping?"

"No, she insisted it was private."

"I'm not surprised. She was pulling the wool over your eyes again to protect him. We all knew of his unwholesome ways before he took off. He was a schemer, that one, and she loved him for it."

Her claim was unthinkable. Ravina had some strange ways, true, but this story of masochism made no sense.

"If there's anyone with an unsavory past, Auntie, it's Algernon. She revealed the ugly story behind why she married him. I can't divulge it. She even asked me to care for him were she to leave, that he was demented. That's what worries me, how she had a premonition."

At that Jemima teetered back in her chair with such force that she almost fell off.

"Ha! Throwing you off again by attacking Algie. Why should he be a threat? He had her—Philip was the one who lost. Did you ever think he got over his bitterness when she so suddenly wed? You didn't know Ravina as I did, more able to watch her grow up. She was attracted to Philip's roguishness. If he hurt her, she was all the more attracted. So many women prefer bad boys. It turned into a very sick relationship once she learned to hurt back."

"Are you implying Philip killed Rebecca? How absurd."

"It would be so easy. Maybe it was accidental. A too-long smother during one of their perverse snogs. He did disappear right away, well before her body was found."

"I refuse to believe any of this fantasy of yours."

"It happens more than the public know. A real kiss of death. Do you know there are clubs in the city where those who favor a bit of rough can practice without fear of dire results? Don't smirk, Eddie. De Sade wasn't just a man of rich imagination. He wrote of what he knew."

"Really, Aunt Jemima, I never expected such perverse gossip from you. You always taught me the straight and narrow. And what about the boat? Explain that for me."

"Simple. He slid her body into it with one sea cock open so it would drift out with the tide and sink."

"Auntie, where did you get this vivid imagination."

"It's no imagining. It's good criminal knowledge from reading mysteries. You should try them sometime, Eddie. You never know when you might want to kill someone."

"I refuse to believe Ravina had those inclinations, let alone that she had relations with Philip."

Jemima laughed until she almost choked. "Of course not, you were in love with her. She was often away, was she not?"

"Charity boards and art classes in London, yes."

"Charity boards! Art classes! Just a disguise for her taboo meetings with others of her odd bend. Ah, I regret you not living in the city when you were younger. There's so much one can't learn from books, well beyond the dalliances you and Freddie enjoy."

I turned to leave, refusing to hear more of her ludicrous "solution" of Ravina's death.

"Hold on, Eddie. Yes, I know about your practices. Gives me chills of delight to think of fashionable ladies baring their spoiled bodies to the butler. All of us are behind you."

"Just what do you mean by *all*?" I spun back.

"Why all of Slyme Gurney of course. Once you freed most servants to live in the village, we had a ready daily bulletin at the pub. The stories are better than any *Ladies Companion* serial. When I moved back with Mr. Poot, the regulars at the pub brought me up to date."

So humiliated, I bade farewell. Aunt Jemima was right. I was naïve. By limiting my life to Slanderley I constructed a prison to keep out larger society. If I missed knowledge of the tawdry, I missed the exultant as well. My youthful folly condemned me to a life of limitation, a well-padded one, one to be envied by a working class laborer, yet a gaol nonetheless.

Each step toward the manor hung an extra chain upon my body, one I could not break, for I was middle-aged with scarce money of my own, and no trade to see my independence. I was enslaved. Marx was correct, except he forgot about us servants, used to having them himself.

Further rumination seemed to prove my Aunt's bizarre theory. Had Ravina been an advocate of de Sade, then Algie's cruel seduction might not have threatened but enticed her. She expected more titillating erotic play, only to learn later she was mistaken. More like *no play* was the result. However unbelievable, her taboo desires, accumulating over time into more risky methods to obtain relief, might have been her concern over "leaving." She wanted me to protect Algie in case she died in some unwholesome ritual.

It now fit! Algie's accusations of women's immorality did base in fact. He was referring to Ravina. Somehow he learned of her deviant ways, from this guest or another who appeared from the city and tattled within his earshot. Now I understood. He needed to erase all memories of his immoral, voluptuous dead wife.

I chose a route to cross the bridge over the gulley, the spot where Charlotte killed herself—or was murdered. My hands shook while I grasped the rail, tremors from my sudden enlightenment. Was Ravina as venal as her predecessor of a century ago? My brain agreed, while my heart refused to listen.

I heard footsteps. It was Freddie, home from London.

Joining me at the bridge, he slapped me on the back.

"Sorry, old chap, I've not taken the Greek ways yet."

It was an old joke between us. He tilted his head, questioning my glum face.

"It's Ravina, haunting me. I've just heard an explanation that casts her in a despicable light, and I daresay it all fits. My sense of reality is smashed." We stared at the rocks below, the creek dragging scraps of twigs.

"I know what you mean—I was fooled too. It wasn't until her death that I changed my views. That is, if she died."

"What do you mean by *if?* You identified the body with Algie."

"What there was of it, you mean. The arms were missing, the breasts gone, the face melted away to skull. All I can say is it was a woman of Ravina's size and build."

"If your supposition is correct, where is she now?"

"Obviously with Philip in Australia. I had insomnia that final evening and was standing on the bridge close to midnight. The water's rustle below soothes me and quiets my thoughts. I glimpsed Philip's car speed by toward the main gate."

"Was Ravina in it?"

"Oh, no, not that I could see. I actually didn't think about this until later."

"I don't understand."

"She could have been riding in the boot. They'd speed to London where she could change her appearance, bleach her hair or something like that. Philip had enough shady connections to counterfeit identity papers and passport. I guess Ravina is holding court at his sheep farm, or more likely at his town house in Sydney."

I almost wanted to believe him, but couldn't. "But what about the boat?"

"That is what clinched me. It was a calm night. She could have taken it into the far end of the lagoon to its deepest point, opened some cocks, and swam ashore. It's the fact the boat never showed up that convinces me she's alive."

"If anyone but you suggested this story, Freddie, I'd call it preposterous. Aunt Jemima has a similarly daft story, that

SLANDERLEY

Philip murdered Ravina, accidentally or on purpose, in some sexual play."

"I'm aware they once had a questionable relationship," Philip replied, "but I think they changed. He was always a bit of a rouser, but he's done well on his sheep ranch down under. Age matured him."

"How do you know this? It's hard to believe."

"I saw Philip anytime our visits to London overlapped, and have written him as well. Don't you know Algie funded his spread in the wilds? I know Philip much better than you. He never forgave himself for being such a roué when he was younger. He had always planned to marry Ravina. But before he could, she accepted Algie."

"Why haven't you told Algie or the police of your ideas?"

"What's to gain? Ravina is gone. They may both be in kangaroo land. Now comes word of Algie's newfound happiness. Whatever has passed we must get on and welcome the new Mrs. De Loverly. Do you know anything about her?"

"No, Algie failed to send so much as her name. Likely a fortune hunter."

"Or she may be more ravishing than Ravina, if that is possible. Someone to obliterate memory of her charm and popularity with even more glitter and elegance. Ravina was, after all, not of high birth. Her adoption was at age thirteen. She played Lady of the Manor but never expressed it to her core. A woman bred for the position would make Ravina seem a poor imitation, which at times she was."

"With a mind like yours, Freddie, it is little wonder of your success. You further confound me, point out my ignorance." I stared into the water below. "Of course, it's clear now: A man with one of the few large homes no debt, no heirs, and no reputation for philandering. A first-rate catch!"

We continued to stare at the torrent without speaking. After a few minutes I asked, "Have you ever thought about Charlotte's death? I do, every time I come by here. Imagine throwing oneself willingly over the edge."

"Really, Eddie, surely she was murdered."

Once again Freddie surprised me. "But there was the letter they found in her room."

"Yet a staff member would have put it there. She wasn't the first to know of its presence. A word, a steaming tea pot, the perfect basis for a crime. Or it could have been a coincidental occurrence, the plan in place independently."

"Suppose you are right. Then what about Lady Gladys, Algie and Letty's mother? Her inquest pronounced suicide as well."

"There are more murderers among us than you conceive, Eddie. I could be one. One can even fancy liking a murderer."

I just shook my head over his latest fantasy. We made our farewell and left in separate directions.

Cutting through woods to the house, I felt layers of loathsome garments drop off me one by one. The cloak of envy, the first-born son condemned by bastardy. The tight shirt of suspicion that bound me from seeing my half-brother as he really was. The hat of misplaced love shading my eyes from

Ravina's true character. The shoes of pigheadedness that marched me down the path of misplaced innocence.

Tears poured down my face in contrition to Algernon. I had never absorbed the consequences of his marriage and Ravina's death. I must shred my gloves of selfishness to provide undying support, from my heart, not out of some promise to our father or Ravina.

A Peace Pact

Preoccupied with my self-loathing, I lost attention of my surroundings. Not that I could see much anyway, given the New Moon. Suddenly the scenery tumbled, trees above me danced, and the sky came to lie on my side, not above.

The odor of fresh cow ordure sent me coughing. Rooks called alarum overhead. I had fallen into a shallow pit, but for what purpose? A snapping of brush nearby grew louder, like drums to an execution.

"Holy Beelzebub, Mr. Quirk! I never expected to bag you. Here, grab my arm and let's go to the garden shed to wash you off."

"Willets—you did this? What is this, a new poaching trap? It doesn't seem practical."

"Naw, it's my latest trick on Mrs. Anvil. She's taken to walking her in evenings. I've hoped she'd fall and spend the night before I 'discovered' her the next morning. It's good you are back, Mr. Quirk. Sorry to give you this sad welcome."

"No trouble at all, Willets. I'm not hurt. It's been a long time. How're things in my absence?"

"Aye, thank you. Things're looking like a jungle here. It Worse inside the manor. Mrs. Anvil's driven off most all the maids. Furniture shrouded. Spiders in all the rooms. She sits in her parlor or shuffles about Ravina's room. Still puts fresh flowers there daily, she does. Even changes the linens according to the mystical thingy. Woman's daft, I say."

"No doubt. I'll have a to-do with her before the newlyweds arrive." While brushing my clothes, he asked, "Will you return to making brandies and cordials, Mr. Quirk? We miss 'em after a hard day in the sun."

"Of course. As soon as the kitchen gardens are cleared out and replanted. But do that first before you go to the berries. I suspect they have overgrown. Meals before tittle."

He handed me a damp rag for my face. "About the azaleas along the drive. Me and Willets have been politely ignoring them, hoping they'd die out."

"Sorry, but we must wait for a specific order. The new lady may prefer them. However, if some bulbs start poking up amidst, I won't complain."

Having cleaned up in the shed, I headed to my apartment to change my ranking clothes and bathe. Leaving all but my underwear in the laundry, I crept up a seldom-used stairwell in the servants' quarters. Halfway up a most discordant sound brayed.

"Well, Mr. Quirk, I'll spare asking how it is you are sneaking about near nude with the smell of barnyard about you. You could have least used clean towels as drapery to keep from frightening the scullery maid. She's the last one to remain living here."

"So I hear, Mrs. Anvil. Not that you have anything to do with the departures, of course."

"Well, I'm not so stupid as to fall into Willet's manure trap. I seen him carting muck into the woods instead of the lettuce bed. Foolish man—like all men."

"I take insult from you as an honor, madam. Now if you'll excuse me, I'm in need of a bath. Would you join me?"

"Disgusting and dirty-minded as always!" she sneered. "Don't think your moonlit tête-a-têtes with visitors fool me. I can't call them ladies. Whores, that's what they are, whores."

"And when did you last try the dance in praise of Astarte, my dear? Oh, don't look so self-pitying. You think it's your scars that drive men away when it's your narrow-minded mean spirit, your disapproval of anyone who enjoys life. And yet—perhaps a creature worth loving still hides within that ugliness. Or so my Christian upbringing insists. But I am a weak Christian."

While I spoke, her eyes opened in disbelief at my challenge. Her hands moved to cover her ears, then turned into fists that pummeled my chest.

"Evil, cruel man, to taunt a cripple! I have nothing, nothing, with Ravina gone. *She* was the only one who loved me."

"I'm not surprised. You each had a sewer for a soul," I sniffed, thinking about what Aunt Jemima and Philip had told me. I didn't want to believe either story, yet the accounts infected my mind nonetheless.

At that I rushed to my suite and slammed the door. After some consideration, I accepted the need to apologize if the household was to run smoothly. With a new mistress arriving, we must develop a united front.

The next day I went into town and bought a costly linen for Mrs. Anvil's private dining table. While she unwrapped the ribbons, I noticed a few brief seconds how her face relaxed to suggest a once adolescent comeliness. Another instant her jaw clenched, the hag returned. What if I had chosen a daintier gift, a cashmere shawl?

My gesture appealing to her temperament, Mrs. Anvil accepted the gift with a nod and sat down so we could arrange the arrival of Algie and bride. I acceded to continuing Ravina's décor and daily schedule until directed otherwise. One major shift was moving the sleeping suites to the opposite wing, for Algie ordered those shared with Ravina closed off. Mrs. Anvil snorted how it was only proper that the second wife get second best, a reference to the smaller draftier chambers. When I did not counter her comment as unkind, she agreed it was time to search out new staff.

We had little time to ensure a return to the earlier, splendid days of the manor. Mrs. Anvil conceded the couple's linens could revert to normal ones of ivory Egyptian cotton. So long as Ravina's rooms remain untouched, she little argued with the removal of some decorative items, which we placed up in the shut-up wing. Yet we forgot exactly what Ravina added to the main rooms and were unsuccessful in keeping all reminders of her out of sight.

Thanks to Freddie's financial success, we catered to Algie's love of tradition. Given the recent recession, which forced economies on other estates, we readily hired staff, some willing to live in as well. Once again they dressed in custom-made uniforms referencing an earlier era. We replaced anything marked with "RdeL" with new ones showing only the family crest. There was money to bring in conservators to clean the best family portraits, the fakes, that is. When the lacquer dissolved, Charlotte's visage shone even more from her place by the new family apartments. We brought from storage the oldest furniture, so different from Ravina's Art Deco aeronautic blond cabinets and bedstead. I presumed the bride shared Algie's traditional preferences.

The day before the couple's expected arrival, Mrs. Anvil and I walked the house together to ensure all our orders had been completed in full. The staff lined up for final inspection, and she caught an uneven hem on one maid, a loose button on a footman. "Spic and span, I want, spic and span!"

I reviewed the daily schedule, a return to Lord Leo's days. The staff relaxed at hearing that, for he had been a late riser. Truth be, with all the new conveniences, the servants had rather light shifts. While they smiled and joked, Mrs. Anvil popped in. "I expect all maids dressed and on duty at six in the morning. I run a tight ship. Spic and span!" Alas, I had no control over the maids' schedule, so they groaned in response.

My duty completed, I wandered into the grounds. I found myself among the old hermitages. Ravina had early reconfigured them into follies. One wall of the Pyramid was exposed to offer a view from inside of the rolling lawn. She and her Mystical friends preferred to sit within, claiming it built up their "auras." By removing the mechanism to open the Snuff Box and glassing its roof, it became a charming hideaway on rainy days. She found the Hedgehog with its rear entrance too outré and ordered it demolished.

I reflected on the many times I'd rolled a cart of tea and biscuits to her at one or the other folly. I envisioned the garden fete where she once again wore the Charlotte dress, this time with hem shortened to appear more contemporary. I struggled to remember her thus, a gracious host and enlivening addition to Slanderley. My early infatuation burst out of my chest, a long neglected alien affection with sharp teeth.

Without meaning to, I slid down the stony path to the beach cottage. That aroused other thoughts, of how Ravina could use her privacy there for purposes other than art. She had created opportunities to meet people unseen. Local gossips, corrupt minds, might spin dark spidery plots of what occurred there.

I shivered and hiked up to the manor for the distraction of dinner. Since we had several new staff residing in quarters, I now ate with them as a way of knowing them better. We had a fine lot. Having left service for offices after the war, they were middle-aged like me. They had the usual names: Anna, Violet, Daisy, James, and Mr. Mosely. I foresaw a smooth operation under Mrs. Anvil, who, I must admit, was an efficient and effective manager of her side.

In my room afterward, I faced my future. Were the bride in any way appealing, I must clamp my emotions from the start. I could not repeat that confused mix of lust and love concerning Ravina. As butler, I was a fulcrum of rationality in the household, a center of calm when hint of a zephyr arose.

The evening before the couple's arrival, I raised a solemn, solitary toast in their honor. I would spend my remaining days in service in penance for my younger stupid and thoughtless ways. I felt Lord Leo pat my back to say, "Yes, my son, you are on the right track again. You will yet become the mature man I saw in you."

The Anonymous Bride

The day arrived, as it must. The weather proffered good omen, there being exceptional sun and warmth, a balminess in the air. Swallows argued over placement of their nests along the eaves of the house. Rhododendrons burst their suicidal bloody red along the wall by the upper drive. Willets disguised the azalea entryway with potted spring bulbs. Despite gardeners' efforts, the long drive in remained overgrown and brambly, a sight likely to lead a childish mind into thinking she was entering a gothic novel.

Alerted by the train master of the couple's arrival at the station, Mrs. Anvil and I lined the staff up outdoors for introduction. We hoped the new bride's spontaneous speech of welcome would make up for Algie's usual Hrumphs. I waited in agitation for the cry of "They're coming!" from a maid set lookout above. Following several deep breaths, I felt a young man again, ready for a fresh start.

I soon heard the motorcar's growl echoing through the woods. As it circled into the main entrance I glimpsed the bride, but caught only a mackintosh pulled before her face as she slunk low in the seat. Algie briefly waved a regal hand.

As I approached to direct the footmen, I opened the door to a very young woman with poorly shorn drab brown hair. Her face lacked any cosmetic enhancements to improve its pleasant plainness. Her coat was too large, perhaps a hand-me-down, her shoe heels worn down, left stocking laddered. Some outmoded ratty marten skins circled her neck. The hint of a dress underneath resembled a potato sack. The effect was that of a little girl playing dress-up from her grandmother's attic.

Then and there my determination to change my ways ended. Seeing her helpless and outclassed, I longed to wrap my arms around her fragile form. I perceived a past not unlike my own, a simple village upbringing, only she had the fortune of her sex to win entry into a magic castle. I envisioned shaping her into a woman of subtle grace and gentle command, who would invigorate the de Loverly line with healthy genes, and none-too-soon, I might add.

Yes, it does not need your pseudo-therapeutic rejoinder to point to my infatuation with my half-brother's wives. Once again I ringed my nose and attached a chain.

While passing by the line of servants, Algie neglected to identify his wife, but simply led her inside. She clung as though he were her Prince Charming, while he responded with the glance of recognition and little pat a man might give his favorite dog. The uninformed would take them to be father and daughter.

Dressed to full effect as the Wicked Witch, Mrs. Anvil stepped in to make a meaningless speech of welcome in her cold rusty voice. Mrs. de L flustered, wrung her gloves, and dropped one. Algie immediately spoke to cover her gaffe, and in an unusually charming manner thanked the housekeeper. He took his wife's elbow and directed her to the stairs and their private rooms.

A jangle of comments tolled among the servants. "A bit young, ain't she? Never saw the master speak so warmly...Did you catch that fur? Like a drowned vole. If that's a lady, I'm Queen Mary....She'd be a darn sight better looking if you put a dab of rouge on her....Never thought the Lord had it in him to catch a looker (that from myopic Widgeon.)

"Silence!" I ordered. "There's time enough after dinner for gossip, though I hope you'll keep civil tongues. We have much to prepare. Check with Mrs. Anvil if you are unsure."

Entering their private lounge with the maid to serve tea, I found Algie poring over a mound of accumulated correspondence, while the wife fidgeted with the hem of her dress. She sat with steady gaze at him, hoping for some acknowledgement. I had to use eyebrows and head nod to communicate she should pour, which she did without inquiring about milk and sugar. She took a cake in her hands and spread crumbs all over her bodice and lap as a result.

Outside Mrs. Anvil cornered me. "What kind of fool does he take us for? She's no better than a scullery maid, so clumsy and nervous, she is. God grants me many burdens, but he tests me mightily with that one! It'll take more than prayer to carry me through."

"Per usual, your vileness rules the day. Just don't go about poisoning the other servants. It's obvious she's from a poor and ill-formed background. But better than two-faced Ravina."

"You, you! Don't ever speak of her that way. No one will take her place here, and as long as I live her memory will survive. Now go get the new missus. I don't think she knows about bath procedure. Doesn't she realize he's work to do after so many months away? And that mackintosh, I plan to burn it."

"Dear Mrs. Anvil," I whispered. "Let's settle down. Leave me in charge of her. Trust me—the worm will turn into a butterfly."

She sneered and hissed back, "More like a moth."

During a brief gathering of staff, I admonished, "Remember the reputation of Slanderley reflects upon us. We can take advantage of the new Lady and play tricks, or we can do as with the Lord, ensure she is in the right time at the place in the right dress, and even suggest the right words. If her behavior brings up a laugh, have the discretion to hide it. Heaven knows, were it not for the potential hilarity, we should be a most dour lot."

Mrs. Anvil barged in all a-tizzy. "She don't want a lady's maid, lacks any sensibility of needing one. Well, I'm calling Mrs. Ogreclap. She has an idle daughter on her hands who is good at playacting. She had everyone laughing at the last village theatre panto."

"I presume she will report everything to you, as well."

Ignoring my barb, she shimmered. "And now *that woman* has Algie so tied up examining honeymoon photographs that

SLANDERLEY

there's to be no change for dinner. She's actually eating in that soiled travel dress. I don't envy the footman who will serve her."

"Couldn't be worse than azalea balm," I chirped while waving her away.

Having tossed my nemesis the final knife, I released the others to check in with Kenneth.

"Certainly a surprise," he acknowledged. "The total opposite of Ravina."

"I take such as hope of a possible relief. I don't see her rushing to order complicated balls and fetes. I wonder whether she's been to a ball in her entire life."

"No doubt that is why Algie was attracted to her. He can start life over by erasing all the old ways."

"Speaking of old ways, as you could see, Mrs. Anvil is in fine fettle."

Kenneth shook his head like a dog whipping off water while wondering aloud why she continued to stay at Slanderley.

I explained, "You'd think she'd have been the first to leave following the discovery of the body, but it was part of the marriage agreement. Ravina wanted assurance of work for life for the old hag. Incidentally, do you know where she went when the house was closed down?"

"She moved into your childhood home, the gatehouse. I think she also took several trips, because there'd be no fire smoke or lights on for weeks at a time."

After passing on more instructions, Kenneth and I went our separate ways. I went down to my apartment, and requested my dinner be brought in there, early if possible. I was unexpectedly exhausted and suffered dreams of rag dolls dancing about the hallways.

My first lengthy encounter with the new wife was next day in the breakfast room. She sat there alone, staring into space while chewing the corner of a linen. Clearly she thought she had nothing to do when there was so much: introductory visits to people of note, dinner invitations to Algie's closest friends, assigning rooms for the next hunt, menus to approve, and most notably, a wardrobe to acquire.

Noticing me, she shrieked a police siren and knocked over the chair as she escaped into the hallway. Kenneth was beyond, blocking her way. He picked up the linen she dropped before him, and bowed. When he stepped aside she dashed into a nearby door, the gun room. You'd have thought we had caught her in a crime.

A few moments later I found her in a saloon, stuffing a box of matches in her pocket.

"May I assist you, milady?"

"Oh, my—I was just—could you give me some matches. The library is chilly, and the fire laid, though not lit."

"Feel free to take the box, however do not light the fire. It is set only if my Lord heads there in the afternoon. There is always a strong fire in the morning room to remove the chill of dawn. The previous wife went there after breakfast to handle her affairs. You may of course use the library if you prefer."

In time she would learn the library was a man's sanctuary, entered by a woman only to select a book or by invitation. Had she ever been a guest at a great house? She seemed a mouse in a trap.

Lady Silly

Turning about, the new wife went passed several doors and entered a cloak room. "Just checking on my coat," she called as she backed out. I followed her slowly behind through the Portrait Gallery. She merely glanced at the paintings, proof further of her ignorance. She wouldn't know a Jacobean from a Georgian, a Van Dyke from a Reynolds, or raw silk from rough hemp.

Eventually she discovered the morning room which looked out upon the sunken garden. Its hall door was open, the hearth ablaze. I pointed her to the desk with its many compartments, flush with pens, writing papers, and record books. I explained the phone had separate lines connected together for convenience, but was in effect not private.

She milled about vaguely, opened and shut the drawers of the other Chinese lacquered cabinet, poked at the vase of fresh azaleas. As I was to advise her once more, the phone rang.

"Slanderley here...I'm sorry, Mrs. de Loverly is deceased...Oh, I'm sorry, Mrs. Anvil...Menu approval? Oh, I didn't realize...Oh, yes, what you believe is best....Sauces? I am not sure, whatever Algernon prefers....Yes, or whatever Ravina might have ordered. Sorry."

I shuddered at her responses. To defer to Mrs. Anvil, to admit weakness, was like serving oneself as lamb to slaughter. When she hung up the phone, I returned to the desk. "This large book, milady, is your calendar. All social events for yourself and his lordship enter there."

"Oh, I don't expect much use of that," she replied. "I am a solitary sort, like Algernon, which is what attracted him so to me. Neither of us needs society."

"That may be your personal preference, milady, but you have duties that require your cooperation. Actually, you will find some entries written in here for you already. There is Boxing Day for the staff, the annual hunt meet, the church fundraising fete, and more."

"Surely we can eliminate some, apart from Boxing Day. I do so enjoy the holiday season."

"Actually not, milady, for Algernon's oldest local friends will expect an invitation to dinner soon."

"Oh, this is more than I ever expected. I don't know how I can manage." She shred several sheets of stationery in the process.

I pulled the pieces from her and continued to explain the different types of stationery and their uses. "There is a useful guide in the library on writing notes of invitation or appreciation. I can bring it to you later."

She slapped her hands in glee. "How lovely! Please do. I need any help you can provide. If it is no trouble."

"Yes, of course, milady. Tomorrow I will go over the manor layout so you can learn about the décor of the guest rooms and which ones have been closed up for convenience."

I wanted to ask her name, but that was not my role. Her willingness to admit ignorance was a good sign though.

Afterward I sought out Mrs. Anvil. She was not happy to see me, yet set herself to listen.

"I was with her ladyship when you called with the menu. She is not yet equipped to handle those selections. Suppose I picked the menu options from you after breakfast. In the morning I'll discuss these with her and answer her questions. I'll call them down so you don't have to deal directly with her."

"That's fully agreeable to me. The less I see of her, the better."

My chicanery thus separated her ladyship from Mrs. Nasty. From that day her ladyship slumped toward the morning room after breakfast as if a dull child going to school.

At week's end Letitia and Reginald arrived to meet their new sister-in-law, yet I could not find her. Thanks to the Cook, I'd learned she had been lurking up a servants' stairwell. "Seems a bit barmy to me. I don't think she's all there, if you catch my point."

When she was nowhere among the service rooms, I returned upstairs. There in the main saloon I discovered Mrs. Anvil, pressing a hand on ladyship's back, directing her toward the Horshams and Algernon. Fingering the collar of her dress with her hand, face white with fear, the wife curtsied before Letitia.

Graciously my half-sister responded with munificent gestures of welcome. "My dear, what a charming dress. I never thought an over-washed print could look so beguiling. How smart that hemline—the length evokes such a pleasing old-fashioned look. Where did you ever find such couture?"

Relaxing in Leticia's graciousness, she answered, "It belonged to the daughter of my employer, Mrs. Cribbage. We were nearly the same size."

"Ah, you've lost weight then? The excitement of the wedding! No matter. You will soon accompany me to London for new clothes, my gift. I am due for some new hunt jackets. Vermillion was the color dear departed Barnaby recommended, the symbol of earnest aggression, just right for my temperament. You will need a hunt jacket as well, though alas Barnaby cannot advise you. He'd suggest violet, I'm sure."

"Hunt, oh, I never—I mean." I thought she'd swoon. "I don't ride. I'm allergic to horsehair. I have to be careful which sofas I sit upon. You never know where it's lurking."

I glimpsed Algie's eyes flicker over this flaw and draw inward. The honeymoon ended then without fanfare. The kindness and concern to all of us upon his return shifted into his normal cool, restrained brooding.

"Perhaps you raise hounds then? Algernon has some ribbon winners, you know. You can assist the hunts that way. What breed might you try?" wondered Letty.

"Oh, I like teeny dogs, not slobbery large ones. I have brought a Yorkie. It's up in my room right now. Its official name is Sir Otis of Glockenspiel the Fourth, but I call him Blocky. Would you like me to have him called down?" She wiggled like a child needing to pee.

"Perhaps another time. If you neither ride nor hunt," puzzled Reginald, "what pleasures you for keeping fit?"

"I walk about and look for unhappy bugs. Isn't it heartbreaking to come upon a beetle on its back? The way they wiggle their teeny legs in the air? I am just drawn to serve them."

"No, my dear, I regret I've missed that pleasure. What I meant was, what do you do for sport?"

"I'm rather fond of the sea. I love to stroke through the waves. Is it safe to swim in the lagoon? From the cliff I saw a charming old cottage. It would make a perfect dressing place. Is that why it's there? Is there a boat as well? It would be so fun to have a picnic with all of us there!"

Algie grimaced. Letitia moaned, astonished by the wife's innocent reminder of Ravina's death."

"Oh, none of you swim?" she asked in innocence.

"We definitely do not, and we do not go to the beach," responded Reginald. "We are country people, not fisher folk."

"Right," added Letitia. "If you are allergic to horses, perhaps you can think about the gardens. They have gone to seed and need some revisions."

"Oh, I don't know." She squinted and crunched her face. "I like the wild look. It brings in more bugs, more beetles to discover. Well, perhaps the kitchen garden can include a lot of those vegetables that attract cabbage moths. I am thinking of turning one of the vacant rooms into a small laboratory where I can study and mount my specimens."

"Ahem, yes, my dear, the old dungeon is now modernized and would serve you well," Algie suggested.

"I can see why Algernon proposed to you," added Letitia. "You have such unusual interests. You will add some vitality to the household."

Overhearing all this from the doorway, I strode in to announce lunch. The party split up to wash, while I stayed behind and went out on the terrace to watch some tits atwitter in the trees.

Letitia found me after lunch. "Really, Eddie, who is she? How trying! Why would Algernon marry a woman with not country ways? Ravina did not hunt, but she was from the duchy. She knew our culture and activities. She never sulked while we were out seeking blood."

"I'm really enjoying the challenge. She's so totally bland and uninformed. I see her as a tabula rasa to fill in with elegant swirls and historic paintings."

"A case of arrested development, you mean. Cabbage moths and beetles. And imagine her mentioning the beach."

"Perhaps Algie never told her the details of Ravina's death. I doubt he has said much about the past at all. As it is, they converse little. He schedules her for dinner hour. We suspect he has yet to visit her bed here."

"That could be. I must try to be sympathetic with the poor thing. But that skirt, and the grease stain down the front. It simply won't do. Most won't give her a second look, if not laugh directly to her face. We must join together on this, Eddie. In the name of Slanderley."

"I value your support. Now head away before others notice we've been talking."

She stayed in place. "I mean really *together*," she purred, and pressed me against the wall. As she ran her hands through my hair and nibbled my neck, I inhaled the scent of Shalimar from her ginger tresses.

"Please, Letty, leave me alone. Go!"

"But when is it *my* turn? You've saved half my friends with their boring marriages. Why not me, your dearest beloved Letty?"

"That would be like incest," I hissed, revealing the truth more than she realized. "I don't want anything to spoil our deep spiritual connection. I won't say the blissful union will never come, Letty, but allow our souls to flower fully first."

"Oh, please write that on a card out so I can keep it under my pillow in anticipation."

And show your slaggy friends, I thought. That moment of treachery conquered, I left for my room to relax with a cigar and newspaper. Instead I fell asleep in my chair.

A rattling at the door shook my luscious slumber. "Mr. Quirk, we need you in the servants' hall. It's an emergency." Anna called.

Another squabble between Mrs. Anvil and Cook I presumed. I sighed, straightened my vest and brushed my coat to delay the inevitable. A surprise on me! The room proved full of congeniality, and Mrs. Anvil was absent.

"We need to know the missus's name. No one recalls hearing it said. You must know what Algie calls his wife," explained Anna.

"Just 'dear.' I haven't heard a Christian name," added James.

"Maybe she ain't got one," guffawed Widgeon.

"Maybe her name *is* Dear," said Violet.

"Hush. We are in a most peculiar spot. Several weeks have passed, yet we lack this essential fact. Algie didn't even use it when Letitia and Reginald visited."

Kenneth introjected, "Therese, you're her maid. What's on her monograms from before? We can try to guess from those."

Therese, actually Molly Ogrecliff, took advantage of a chronic sinus infection to enhance her French accent. "I hate to describe her oondergarmahnt. Bah! She should be handling and repairing my clothes. Monograms? She is fortunahble to have labels."

"I suggest we make up a code name for downstairs," mused Mrs. Viscous.

There followed chatter and argument over the choice. Mary—too plain. Hermione—too much personality. Elizabeth—too regal. Jean—all accepted. Then Kenneth recalled one of the village day maids had that name.

To stop the quibbling, I advised we draw one from a lot, each person entering a name yet to be discussed. Violet plunged her scrawny hand into the chosen milk bucket and withdrew the prize sheet. Unfolding it, she whined like a sick hawk."

"What is it?"

"I can't read."

Grabbing the sheet, I pronounced 'Cecily.'"

"That's mine," smiled Mrs. Quinceprick. "I always wanted a daughter named Cecily but didn't meet Tom here until I was too old. Still, I can't say I'd want my Cecily to turn out like that one," pointing a knife upstairs. "Such a dormouse. Oh, for the days of Ravina, demanding though she was."

"Ce-CIL-y?" Therese screwed up her nose in bad French.

"Silly, yes," jumped in Kenneth. "Not C*e*cily, but Ce*silly.*"

A Slothful Tale

One night Sloth mentioned over dinner how he'd run into Cesilly at the beach cottage. Any self-respecting estate needs an imbecile, and lacking a real one, Sloth enthusiastically enacted such to the upstairs folk, perfecting his part with a slobber from the left corner of his mouth and a lazy right eye. His favorite attack was scaring guests on walks.

"I were digging for shells, when she come along with that frou-frou dog she now keeps, who barked and snapped at me. Nasty mop. When she thought I wasn't looking, she went into the cottage. I peeked in and watched her poke about Ravina's paintings and things. I decided t'would be fun to scare her a bit. Went in and moaned, 'She's gone to sea. None like her. She'll return one day, just you see.' Her lady rushed out by me screaming while I cackled back." Sloth added one of his goofy sounds to remind us.

"I followed behind and saw her partway up the cliff path, Algie yelling at her. He reminded her the beach was a forbidden place. She said she were walking her dog and it pulled her down the path, how she didn't mean to go there. Algie turned, face scarlet, and cursed aloud how he should never have returned to Slanderley."

Sloth went on to discuss how she struggled up the stone walk to catch up, all the time shouting, "I didn't mean it, I didn't."

Knowing of Algie's rare yet beastly temper, we wondered the long term consequences of this encounter. Typical of servant talk, we each had a separate opinion and spent the next hour tossing ideas. In the end we agreed life was a lot more interesting with Cesilly, however queerly she acted. Plus we had much less work.

The next day I went to see Freddie and share Sloth's story. I knew he'd want the good laugh.

"I expect you want to tell me about the new wife, but I've already had a long talk with her," he said while pouring drinks.

"How is that possible? You've been so busy catching up with your paperwork here after London. And by the way, the staff now refers to her as Cesilly, given we still lack her given name."

"She stopped by late yesterday afternoon. She was on a walk and noticed me by the bridge. I explained my position and invited her in for tea. She fretted that Mrs. Crabnoggin described the annual costume ball and urged her set a date for the next one. I emphasized how important it was, that her role was to go over the old guest list and eliminate those who had died. A temporary secretary would handwrite the invitations for her to sign. She relaxed some and even accepted a glass of sherry."

He refilled our brandy sniffers and smiled before continuing on. "She stared into the hearth and described how Sloth scared her earlier at the beach cottage. She asked about Ravina, the cause of her death. I provided the basic details, my identification of the body, and Algie's despair."

"She teared up a bit and ran on how she was no match for Ravina. She confessed embarrassment over her clumsiness and lack of grace. She said she should never have accepted Algie's proposal, being ignorant of the requirements of Lady of the Manor. Discovering how Ravina filled the position with such élan added to her sense of incompetence."

"How did that confession hit you?"

"I couldn't decide whether she was genuinely guileless or one of the wiliest women to ingratiate me so. I felt cornered by a harmless rabbit, and couldn't tell why. I assured her not to feel inadequate, that modesty trumped beauty. I said so ironically, but she didn't catch my tone, and insisted I describe Ravina. Which I did in full, her many virtues included. You know me, unable to resist an opportunity to be a bit smart."

"You overextended yourself this time, Freddie. Did she tell you that Algie caught sight of her on the beach? How her screaming at Sloth drew his attention outside to see her?"

"No. What happened?"

"Apparently he cursed her for disobeying him, and she groveled up the cliff to seek forgiveness. She really loves him, Freddie. You cannot compare Ravina in full maturity to a girl who has yet to acquire her full character."

"Really? Consider what type of woman would marry a well-placed man in mourning in circumstances where he was away from friends and advisors. Even if she is naïve, why dash into marriage recklessly? Why did she avoid a proper introduction to his family?"

"Your lack of knowledge of women is showing, Freddie. This is still a girl, about to flower. Rather, we must ask what has caused her to be so meek and docile, this at an age when most young women are plucky and out-going."

Pausing for Freddie poke the fire, I continued. "I've thought much about this, and have a sense of her origins. Second daughter, not quite wanted, of an older couple, Methodists no doubt. On the fringes of a good family line, the branch from a ne'er-do-well. A suburban home with those scratchy brown velour overstuffed sofas with crocheted doilies. Father, a minor town official, smokes pie and reads paper in the evenings, while mother darns socks. Talk is meaningless commentary on local affairs and gossip. Older sister, a strawberry blonde with long inviting legs is bright, friendly, and fun. Parents dote on her. Little Cesilly, scrawny for her age, is vaguely acknowledged. Dressed in hand-me-downs, she never develops self-expression.

"Having spent too many nights reading florid romances, Cesilly signs on with an agency, thinking that serving as a companion, like governesses of mouldy novels, will link her with a Prince Charming. A wealthy widow engages her for a Continental tour. In Monte Carlo, they meet Algie, who is irresistibly drawn to Cesilly's quiet manner, the opposite of

Ravina in every way. On impulse, he proposes. Her dream having come true, she hasn't the ability to refuse."

Freddie laughed while responding. "There goes your literary imagination full steam. Turn it into a novel. How could the companion of a wealthy woman so lack in basic social grace."

"Her employer was American."

"True, she'd never acquire posh from a Yank."

"I'm ready to bet five pounds my interpretation is correct. Let's check on her. Is it a deal?"

"How, Eddie, can we find out when we don't know her actual name?"

"Tell Algie you need the marriage notice for family records. Then employ an investigator to make inquiries. I'm sure her story is quite as I imagine, even duller."

"Engage a snoop? Eddie, how immoral. Actually it would be good for the estate. I've been urging Algie to update his will, and while he needn't know, the solicitors would be grateful to know of potential claims from her family in the unlikely event—"

"That both die at once."

"Precisely. Which suggests another puzzle. If she has a family, why haven't they been notified and invited here to meet him?"

"Perhaps she is alienated, or cut herself off from them."

"You make a good case, Eddie. Here you live midst a small community, where everyone knows the others' foibles, and while mocking them, rest secure that all are known. The grocer lays his thumb on the scale, Mrs. Viscous pockets money for a few more hams than meet the table, our Bishop's wife cannot keep a confidence, our doctor shows himself to little girls. None are fully trustworthy or moral, but we know enough to act accordingly. Since our faults are common knowledge, we can trade and converse as equals. We are generous and tolerant, though a stranger overhearing gossip might think otherwise."

I teased back, "So now you are a sociologist." He ignored my jibe.

"In the city, where I spend much time, maneuvering for one's place prevails. Identities can be elaborated, invented, without disclosure. Proper clothes and the right accent may be keys to all but the highest circles. One didn't go to Harrow, one explains, because one's father was in obscure duty in South Africa. The listener registers 'Harrow,' and by week's end you have a graduation class. Anonymity supports fabrication and dissembling. As in my case, my covering of my own illegal activity."

"Your Wildean inclinations should not be a crime."

"True, but my point is this. People can get away with the most outrageous acts: larceny, espionage, blackmail, and kiddie-tiddling."

He tapped his pipe, set at me with a gleam in his eye, and whispered, "Murder, you never know when there's a murderer in one's midst. Even I could be one."

It was so like Freddie, an amateur actor in his school days to close this claptrap with that dramatic touch. I grabbed the poker, raised it, and mocked back, "Me too!"

I left my friend in an expansive mode, having obtained his promise to be kinder to Cesilly. We reaffirmed our main service was to Algie, which required soothing and guiding her.

Nothing could shake my high spirit, even the fog horns mourning their eternal reminder of sailors gone to deep.

Tittle-Tattle

Alas, the new mistress proved true to her downstairs nickname. I wish I could report we in service were compassionate. If we held back our titters, we couldn't resist a blather over her gaffes. She splotched the heavy correspondence paper, curtsied to untitled Mrs.Crabnoggin, and still refused help with her bath. Her demands few, they little made up for our vigilant surveillance to prevent another public *faux pas*.

Letitia kept her promise to help transform the toad into the princess. However, she was unable to interest her in a new wardrobe, nor get her to a doctor who could cure her allergy to horses. Frustrated, she turned to simpler changes.

Letty reviewed old guest books with Cesilly to discuss the personalities of future visitors. "It is important that you know several facts about each to participate in a conversation. It's like being the Queen in a way. *You* start the discussion,"

She had Cesilly write out cards on each person to study afterward and tested her later, with little success.

"Mrs. Herbdixon, short with blond hair, raises Pomeranians and hates vegetarians," asserted Cesilly.

"No, Mrs. Herblexicon, short with black hair, raises Shetland ponies and hates vegetables," corrected Letty.

Letty concluded it would be a long, long year of training. In the meantime the two of us would need to whisper in Cesilly's ear at appropriate moments of introduction or discussion.

She explained the afternoon tea ritual, which led to similar mixed results. "Your cup is not a ball—don't clutch it with both hands….That's better, but don't stick your index finger through the handle. See how delicately I take hold? Now try to stir….No clinking! And don't make a whirlwind."

Moving on to the serving of tea to guests proved so beyond Cesilly's ken that Letty decided to be pourer. Instead she gave Cesilly control of the coffee urn, for the bitter bean was becoming a preference of those guests who fancied themselves *au courant*. (I so love French.) Twice a month Letty brought a carefully selected well-wishers by to develop Cesilly's manners in this regard.

At least she knew how to eat dinner, thanks to the training from her previous employer in Monte Carlo. Which is not to say finger bowls and wine glasses remained stable at her setting.

With each gong of the doorbell, her intimidated ladyship dashed to her bedroom, were she not already hiding there. When called, she appeared dejectedly in her ill-fitting jumpers and skirts, woolen stockings sagging about her ankles. They ran the array of brown shades, from mud to old cigar.

If Algie joined the gathering, Cesilly sat like a nervous school girl. In his absence, she mispronounced names and spilled coffee on others' laps. Trapped in her insecurities, she neglected how visitors of lesser rank arrived no more secure, that they expected her to put them at ease. Worse, she seldom inquired of other's interests and predilections. Her sentences went "Algernon always says...Algernon disapproves of...." and similar cant.

Strangely, her gaucheness produced a favorable reputation those who preferred women in their submissive place. Because this Lady of the Manor was not a dazzler in dress or jewelry, husbands appreciated their wives would not beg for money to compete. Shy wives left feeling superior. True, some left murmuring uncomplimentary comparisons to Ravina. What most visitors missed was that deceased woman's vitality and fun, as well as her acts of charity.

In time both upstairs and downstairs viewed Cesilly as a daft cousin, a well-meaning bumbler. The clincher was her bug museum. Close to a year into her reign, she had furnished the old dungeon with a study table, microscopes, and glass top cases designed to display her neatly labelled specimens. There she oozed to guests over her live black bean aphids sucking on a branch, along with dead and pinned gorse shield bugs and common froghoppers. Once word spread of this hobby, well-bred visitors filed her away as another loveable British eccentric.

Despite Letitia's efforts, I could do little with regard to the hunt and duchy-wide events held like clockwork at Slanderley. Cesilly told me she must protect Algie, how "he is in mourning and not ready for big social activities. Perhaps in a year or two." Apart from Letty's appearances and a necessary dinner for one of Algie's friends, the house seldom echoed with wit.

Meanwhile I tried to foster Cesilly's good will. I pulled out a book listing local families in need of charity. "It is even more important during these hard times to visit these cottages and take along some produce. See here, the Greckle family, with crippled tiny Tim. Just the tiniest gift will mean so much." Even then she demurred that she must not leave the house in case Algie needed her. In the meantime I visited the hovels or had baskets sent over.

I continued to sit with Cesilly in the mornings to continue mentoring. She was not always slow in grasping an idea, yet once conquered soon seemed to forget. I couldn't determine whether she had a poor memory or wasn't focusing on the work. Her eyes at times belied intelligence when she was off on her own in the garden or reading a book of etymology.

Summer sloshed by. Birds quieted in molt. Bugs basked in steamy sunny interludes between showers. Rhododendrons dropped their flowery wounds to wrap up in neurotic security along the walls. Willets informed me the unusual heat and humidity was knocking off the more fragile strains of azalea, a rare sign of hope.

I wish I could report the strains between Cesilly and Algie had mended, that they were in a predictable state of post-honeymoon disillusionment. Alas, no. There was no shouting, no slamming of doors, no broken plates. Rather, the marks were well-disguised, like animal tracings in a leaf-strewn wood, apparent to only the most perceptive eye.

Thus I kept a tally. If Cesilly rushed in early for breakfast one day to sit with her husband, Algie found reason to eat even earlier the next. "Oh, my dear, what a shame! I must check some traps with Quinceprick this morning before the showers strike. Do enjoy your breakfast. Perhaps you can order some French omelets in the future. Ravina so loved them. A change from my porridge?" He delivered such with charm, yet the irony was clear to me.

I might hear him drop a criticism over diner. "My dearest, Mrs. von Biddenbane feels abused by your failure to call on her. I thought you were doing better, but Widgeon informs me you order him to drive about the countryside rather than meet your social obligations. As mistress of Slanderley, they are small coin for your privileges. I know Mr. Quirk guides you concerning these appointments. Do attend to Ravina's notes."

If harsh on paper, again the words passed with a silver tone, a pat upon her hand. The admonition, however mild, concluded with an abrupt, "You must excuse me tonight, dear, to look over important business with Freddie. I'm sure you can entertain yourself sufficiently."

It was painful to watch. In spite of being gauche and sometimes disobedient, during such brief encounters Cesilly fawned over and reassured him. "Sorry, so sorry, my dear, you know I am very shy. Sorry. Just as you prefer your solitary times, so do I. It is what we have so much in common, our respect for one another's privacy. And I thought it too early to be social when the house is still in the formal period of mourning."

He looked up in surprise. "I hadn't thought of that."

"My dear, you have so much to worry you since you returned. I know I am disappointing you, but promise to do better. I'm so sorry."

Such talk seemed to soothe him, though I wondered whether it fully quelled his concerns. I knew he went to the windows several times a day to ascertain she had not gone down again to the beach. Or was he recalling the lost wonderful times with Ravina?

Anvil Omens

One late summer day I entered the kitchen to confront a skirmish between Mrs. Anvil and Kenneth.

"You did it—who else could have?" she growled. "You were the last one in the morning room before it was found. I just know you knocked it down, you clumsy oaf! That little porcelain was worth several years of your wages. I'm going to call the constable. You deserve to be locked up for this one."

"I don't know what you are talking about. I've broken nothing, and had I done so, I wouldn't hide it. I'd have brought it for repair. Remember when his lordship tossed the fruit bowl at Willets? You yourself sent me to the mender in London. Cut into my holiday too with not so much as a Ta."

"Don't play your logic games with me. I know you siphon petrol off the estate car and give some to your friends at the pub. You're a cheat and liar, through and through. You're due for the nick."

Kenneth grabbed a cup and smashed it on the table. "There, if you think I break pottery, I'll do it in front of you."

As he reached for a plate, I grabbed his arm. "Hold on there, both of you. Kenneth, you go to the silver safe and put some of that anger into polishing tea sets."

He turned to me. "But I didn't do it. This bloody witch—"

"How could you let him go like that," shrieked Mrs. Anvil. "The maid saw him leave the room just before she went in and made the discovery."

"I'm not sure that's proof," I asserted. "Just what was broken anyway?"

"That statue of Pan on Ravina's desk."

"Not so terrible a loss. A copy she brought along when she married. And it's no longer Ravina's desk, Mrs. Anvil."

I reported the incident to Algie during tea. "I'm sure Kenneth is innocent," I advised. Cesilly began to stir her cup with such a fury that the drink sloshed over onto her less ugly grey tweed skirt. Upon leaving, I took my post by the door.

Cesilly's wriggled in her seat, then stood up to approach Algernon. "I'm so sorry. I'm the one who broke the Pan. I knocked it over when I stood up from the desk. After picking up the pieces, I stuffed them in the flower vase, unaware the maid had not changed the day's blooms. I'd hoped to find a suitable replacement in the village."

"Why sneak like that? I don't understand," Algie replied.

"I was afraid of what Mrs. Anvil would say."

His voice rose. "Defer to the housekeeper? What are you thinking?"

I could catch only his voice during the softer interchange that followed. So use your imagination as to Cesilly's side, as I had to do.

"Think you ill-dressed? Not at all....The Pan didn't mean a thing to me....No, it wasn't my mother's....Yes, it was Ravina's. She had a good eye....Hardly! No, I'm not bored. I was just wondering whether my new hound will prove a good bitch." Then he left.

I knew Algie's words to be lies. He did care about Cesilly's lack of style. He did admire Ravina's porcelain Pan. Now he was caught in a tragic bond to an irresponsible young woman who seemed intent on continually irritating old wounds, however by accident or ignorance. The new bitch hound would never harm him.

The next day he went to London to attend some events he normally avoided. When he called daily to check on things, I would ask, "Shall I call her ladyship?" to which he always said, "No bother, just say I am well."

His departure oddly lifted Cesilly's mood. She was a colt free to run free for the first time. Wandering about, she sang odd little folk tunes, even Welsh ones, stole sweets from the kitchen as if daring to be caught, and even smiled once at Mrs. Anvil. Only weeks later would this change of mood reveal its significance. Yet for me dark descended, trapping me in a sense of murderous intrigue.

A threat to Cesilly came through an unwanted guest. I was immersed in some enchanting Victorian photography of a somewhat indelicate nature when downstairs maid Clementine waddled into my sitting room without knocking.

"For heaven's sake, girl, where's your manners?"

"Forgive me, Mr. Quirk. I'm sorry, but, well, something awful is going on and, sorry, I just had to rush in and tell you."

"Is it his lordship? Is he alright?"

SLANDERLEY

"No nothing like that. Mr. Phillip Elmsby is in the drawing room with Mrs. Anvil. I seen him myself. They're fighting something dreadful. I know his lordship wouldn't stand for his presence here."

I pushed her aside and rushed over to the saloon. The door was open, so I snuck into a side chamber.

Philip's voice was shaking. "Leave this to me! Keep out of it—it's my revenge."

"Calm down, Philip. You aren't being fair. I'm in this with you as I have always been. I won't leave you with the sole burden. If you are caught, I shall go down with you, for Ravina's sake."

I heard him light a cigarette. "You're right. I'm being too heroic. You deserve some share of the sweet pleasure of punishment."

"So we go as originally planned, get rid of her first?"

"Yes, and strike him when least prepared." His voice changed as if aware someone were listening. "How now, what's this? Brambles? Why are you nosing me?"

He followed the dog down the hall, unaware of my hiding nearby. "Well, hallo there. You must be the new Mrs. de Loverly. Algie sure knows how to pick the lookers. Philip Elmsby here, an old friend of the family, come to see Mrs. Anvil. Quite a good lady and another old friend."

"How do you do?" He wore his usual natty style and flashed his snowy teeth. "I was walking toward the saloon when Brambles ran off to the sound of your voices. Not recognizing yours, to tell the truth I turned back in case you were an appointment I'd forgotten. I don't have a very good memory."

Mrs. Anvil approached and broke in. "Come Philip, I doubt my lady wishes your company. You know better than to intrude during my working hours."

"Not at all," chirped Cesilly. "I should be grateful if you would join me for tea, Mr. Elmsby. I have not had many visitors."

"Your invitation is hard to resist, but I am overdue in Chew Kewsbarrow and must get on the road immediately. Perhaps another time? May I ask, where's Algernon?"

"He's gone down to London to his club. So do return when he is here. I'm sure he will be sorry to have missed you."

"My bad luck again. You see, I moved to Australia, stopped for a quick look-in. Algernon should know better than to leave you unchaperoned. Someone may carry you off." He laughed heartily, and Cesilly actually joined in.

The spider set his trap well, with Cesilly a moth off to a beacon. "Well, may I walk you to your car?"

"What a kind gesture. I'll be writing, Anvy, old girl."

"Where is your car? I don't recall hearing any come in the circle."

"Down by the rhododendron wall. Didn't want to wake anyone having a nap. My motor's quite loud. Mrs. Anvil knew I was coming."

Soon they were out of earshot. It was many minutes before I heard the engine start up in the distance. I fretted each minute they were together, leisure for him to quiz and study his prey. She confounded me, but now I moved further in her defense.

The second threat occurred the next afternoon. I glimpsed Cesilly check to be sure no one was looking and rush quietly up the stairs to the closed wing with the old family apartments. I waited before using a servant stairwell into the same area. The sea nearby beat its mournful tattoo on the beach in time with my heart, wild with some primordial fear over the musky, decaying odor in this once glorious marital suite.

The door to Ravina's was open. I peeped to see Cesilly rustle the bedspread, open the closet doors to finger the sumptuous wardrobe, examine the ivory boudoir set, puzzle over the Mystic Hues altar in the corner. I was about to enter when I heard other steps on the stairwell. The adjoining dressing chamber held a peep hole, so an interested husband could check upon his wife's state before entering. From its vantage I espied the most extraordinary demonic ritual.

Mrs. Anvil entered regally and grabbed Cesilly's arm. She pulled her about the room, introducing Ravina's private effects, from perfume to shoes and lingerie, commenting on each with rapturous praise. Even a dolt could not miss the intended humiliation. Cesilly kept mute.

"Feel this silk? She bought only the best. Like baby's skin. And this shoe, small as a cat's foot. You'd get not a toe into it. I can hear her today, calling for her chartreuse panties, the ones for the 15th of the month. Such refinement! Algernon adored her, you know. He begged me to clip a lock to keep in his shaving drawer." With that remark she snipped a nail shears within a wisp of Cesilly's nose.

If her ladyship had any doubt of Mrs. Anvil's cruelty, it vanished when the wretch took both arms, pushed her toward a tall casement window and shook her. "She had nothing on when they found her. Her arms were torn away. Some days I scour the beach expecting one to return, to see once more those dainty hands with cherry pink polish on the nails. Oh, how I wish!" She shoved her captive hard against the window. When she let go, Cesilly's arms held bone-white spots where the vile fingers had gripped.

"Ah, but it doesn't matter. She's still here, can't you tell? I see her changing her panties with the lilt of a faerie sprite. Sometimes I feel the heat of her breath on my neck in the morning room, that rosemary dentifrice. I wonder, do you think she peeks in when you and his lordship are, well,--"

"Go away," whined Cesilly. "I don't know. I don't want to know."

"Must give her quite a start to see you throbbing where she should lie. Or are the servants correct, that your bed remains unsullied? Well, tea-time. That's what I am here for, to call you down."

She spun and swept away, while I stood soaked in sweat. Mrs. Anvil's actions affirmed the nefarious plan she had made with Philip Elmsby. First, she would torture, perhaps to provoke a suicide and keep their hands clean.

A third episode sealed my fears. Late that night I was in the servants quarters alone, testing my latest cordial mix.

"Hallo, Mr. Quirk. Mind's if I join you? Spent a good day moving rocks and could use a pick-me-up."

"Please do, Sloth."

"Aye, thank you," he replied, warming his hands on the fire. "Had a good joke with her ladyship today, if I saw so myself. 'Twas by the beach with my fishing gear, poking about my storage. She may not have known it were my stuff. She called me out for taking other people's things, like a barmy school mistress. Well I just shook and started to cry like a boy caught with his dad's best pipe. 'You aren't going to lock me up, are you?' I cried. I fell on my knees and slobbered on her hand. To add the final touch I said, 'You aren't at all like the other one, the one that went away, the beauty.'"

"Sloth, wasn't that a mite cruel?"

"Naw. You see she suddenly grabbed my shoulders and screamed that I had never seen her there, down on the beach. If I ever told of seeing her, she'd have me locked up at one of those places for nutters on the moor. She said they'd chain me up and make me sleep on straw. So I begged her pardon."

"She talked back to you? That's odd. She's usually so timid."

"Maybe so, but I saw vengeance in her eyes, accusing me of being an evil doer."

Later I realized Cesilly was protecting herself from Algie's terror had he learned she disobeyed him about the beach. Could she only know her real enemies! Algie's threats were puff of smoke compared to those other two. I needed Sloth's help, so I drummed up a deceptive plan.

The next day, I found him preparing a rabbit trap and gave him a bottle of brandy. "It's for a favor. For the nonce, please, keep an eye on her ladyship without her knowing. We must learn if she is up to something. His lordship forbade her to go to the beach, so why was she there? What is she doing when she is not inside? I need to know so I can develop her freetime schedule, in case I need to find her, that is."

"Be a snoop, you mean."

"Yes, but just between us. This morning her ladyship told me she was looking out her window and was frightened to see a hare with fiery eyes. You know what that means." I whispered, "*The curse of Slanderley has returned.*"

Sloth moaned when I stated the last.

It was of course a reference to the abbess at the convent in Gimunderford-upon-Withover. Upon her blessed deathbed she damned Algernon's great-great Uncle Albert for deserting her in the Wookie Hole caverns during a spoon when they were teenagers. She had tempted him there to donate her virginity. The horror over his humiliating refusal led her to flee to the veil, a choice she and her hapless charges regretted ever after. "Since you failed my dreams, Lord Albert, to stick it up me, I shall return to stick it up your kin and all who associate with you for generations to come." Then she called the Bishop, confessed her uncharitable outburst, and died sinless in the comfort that absolution could not cancel her haunting oath.

But I digress. The reference to the curse was to misdirect Sloth, a superstitious sort, and distract him from further questions about Cesilly. He became what I needed most, a vigilant assistant, whose ignorance aided my counterstrategies. If Sloth knew my lie, so soon would half of Slyme Gurney, who believed fiery-eyed hares to be the devil incarnate. This assault must be led by a single general, *moi*, with aid of an unwitting army.

Swept Away Again

A week later Algie called to announce his expected return from London, that I inform Cesilly for him. She must have overheard the ring. Before I could find her, she rushed to the phone closet, expecting him to be on the line. Returning in a sulk, Brambles ambled over and Lucy plopped atop her feet. How oddly attracted the dogs were to her, more than her own yapper Glocky.

Which reminds me, that infernal mop on legs was typical of its stubborn breed. Being a permissive mistress, Cesilly ensured it never became fully trained. Discovering little gifts and puddles about the house did not endear the staff. If I noticed Glocky out of her room I cleaned after it before a maid came upon the "presents." Its other Yorkie quality was its sheer devotion to Cesilly, which led to nipping and yapping at the rest of us.

I turned to her while kicking my feet at the cur. "Sorry, my lady, but his lordship was calling during a break while attending a lecture about boar hunting." When she looked up I realized she had cosmetics on her face. Given her unpracticed hand, she resembled an aging cinema star: rosebud lips, bruised eyes, perky cheeks.

Sulking, she shambled off toward the main saloon. Before I could leave the phone closet, a new rang made me answer. It was Letitia on line. "Eddie, I thought I would take her Lady to Nan's. It's time they met."

"You mean they haven't been introduced yet? I thought that happened already during one of your visits out together."

"Not at all. Perhaps Algernon couldn't bring himself to introduce his little waif. Nan so loved Ravina. This one is such a puzzling creature. Anyway, you know Nan's inner eye. She can grasp character in a minute without seeing them."

"Fine, you watch. Cesilly will manage to break half the tea set before she sits down. Shall I bring her to the phone or shall you call later?"

"Now, please. It's arranged for this afternoon. I'll explain the plans while you go ahead to Nan's to prepare things. Stop at Slyme Gurney to pick up her favorite biscuits, and I'll bring cucumber sandwiches. I'll tell our little charge you'll serve there because Nan's staff have the afternoon off."

Laying the phone down, I fancied I heard the click of a receiver. Mrs. Anvil no doubt. Well, two could play the same game.

I rushed on my motor bike to the village and then to Chilsworth. When I arrived Nan was taking her post-lunch nap, so Rose and I retired to her quilts. After remaking our acquaintance I filled her in on the strange goings on and my belief Ravina might be alive in Australia.

"Though your idea could make sense, Eddie, I don't understand your new view of Ravina. You used to follow her like a nursing puppy. If flighty at times, and with strange preferences, her heart was golden. No, I can't imagine her fleeing with Philip. A sad accident, that's all. No mystery. Just as I think you read too much into the latest tiffs. New couples have growing pains, not that you would know. You lack understanding of lovers' passing storms."

"Do I detect a wisp of rancor in that remark?"

"More than a wisp, as you so delicately put it. You know, they say butlers grow to resemble their masters. You're so blind to what's going on around you that you pen little dramas in your mind rather than face facts. I needn't mention that you can be as cool and unconcerned as he often is." She pulled her wrap around tight and began to slip on her stockings.

"I confess to being less than devoted to you. You've a right to be disappointed, even angry. Of all the women I've known, I should have sought your hand years ago. But as for fantasizing events at Slanderley, I draw the line. What about the conversation between Philip and Mrs. Anvil?"

"You are so charmingly naïve, Eddie. Most of your information is eavesdropping. You don't see and hear everything. Mrs. Anvil was with the Elmsbys for years before joining Slanderley. Isn't it more likely she and Philip are settling some shady deal from the past? Have you a shred of evidence a real plot against Algernon and Cesilly exists? Were names mentioned?"

"Not precisely, but—"

"See what I mean. Flights of fancy."

"What of Mrs. Anvil tormenting Cesilly in Ravina's bedroom?"

"That's easily explained. Mrs. Anvil is frustrated. She used to be in the center of daily activities, hearing Ravina's confidences, sharing in the plans for parties, enjoying glamour secondhand she never knew herself. Now she's boxed in with a creature who pouts about all day and adds to the manor's gloom. I think she was trying to badger Cesilly to get moving and make a name for herself. You're so busy protecting that you can't see beyond your nose. You are the one who needs protecting."

"Why I believe there's jealousy in that remark," I teased, while reaching for Rose's waist.

She shoved me away. "For God's sake, Eddie. Can't you see you're in love with her?"

Her comment stung like a whip. Could it be true? Then why did I spend my days lurking about, spying on Cesilly, and looking for signs of danger? Before I could answer, a cane knocked the door.

"Come on, you two. Ready for tea. Rose, I need your help with my dress. My wrists are too stiff today."

While I prepared refreshments in the pantry, I heard Letty and Cesilly arrive and join Nan on the veranda. Rills of conversation fluttered by, mentions of Algie, Italy, wedding presents. I entered as though facing a stage. Rose sat knitting beside Nan, whose eyes stared unfocused in the distance while she raised one unrelated question after another. Cesilly was hunched over, playing with the hem of her skirt, responding in monosyllables. Letty gestured animatedly like an orchestra conductor trying to bring two soloists together.

At one point Cesilly spilled her sandwich plate onto the floor, shattering it into slivers. "No bother," assured Nan. "It was one of my newer dishes, from my great-great-grandmother's bridal set." In her haste to sweep up, Cesilly upended her chair, crashing it against Nan's legs. Letty pulled Cesilly into another one, and motioned for me to clean up.

"You must be tired from your trip to Italy," tinkled Nan.

"I've been back several months."

"Really? Well, some people are slower to adapt than others. How long are you planning to stay at Slanderley?"

Letty jumped in. "What a funny question, Nan. Slanderley is her home."

"Oh, you're a relative of Ravina's? A cousin she asked to stay? Or are you the new secretary?"

"No, Nan, she's Algernon's new wife."

"Yes," added Rose. "Remember the day I read the letter from Italy?"

"How can that be? Is Algernon a bigamist? Where is he? Why hasn't Ravina come with you?"

"Ravina is dead," reminded Rose.

"What do you mean? That can't be! I want Ravina. Why are you all keeping her away?"

"Rose placed her hands on Nan's shoulders. "You seem tired. Shall we go in? I'll fix you a nice warm cider."

Nan stood up and moved toward Letty. "I don't know what kind of trick this is, but I don't like it. Next time bring Ravina."

Poor Cesilly sat like a basset downcast in humiliation over a lost scent. I whispered, "Don't take this personally, my lady. She's had a difficult day. I'm sure you'll find a note of apology in the next post." She looked up at me, her large doe eyes warm and dewy in gratitude.

Letty led her out while I finished up in the kitchen. "Rose, what do you think that was all about? You know as well as I Nan was feigning senility. Why was she so cruel?"

"She whispered the girl is either a fool or a fraud. She can't abide that mousy attitude, and neither can I."

"So smug and quick to judge," I sputtered. "So full of innuendoes. Apart from Letty, everyone conspires and laughs when she falls into traps."

"But she is such a fool. Why are you defending her?"

"Trust me, Rose. She needs protection."

"Trust you?" She slapped her towel on the counter. "It's clear you are befogged again, the way you were with Ravina."

She came up close, and I opened my arms to embrace her. Instead she slapped my face. "You don't have to worry about me and my disagreeable attitudes any longer. I gave my notice last week and leave for the Dover at the end of the month. Nan's flow of temporaries will keep you satisfied, no doubt."

"Rose, I wish you wouldn't leave it this way."

"You had your chance, Eddie. But once that fool arrived at Slanderley, you forgot either Nan or I was alive. Keep dreaming. I'll take this world."

On the ride back I cut over the fork to Freddie's cottage. He was standing on the far end of the Charlotte death bridge, tossing crumbs to Pekin Ducks below.

"Eddie, you must have read my mind. The report came in. On her ladyship. The detective's findings."

I was thrown back. Something in me resisted wanting to know of her past. It was her presence I now adored. "Oh, Freddie, you really went through with my joke?"

"Well, it was a smart idea anyway. Here's your fiver for being right. Your hunches were pretty close to the mark. Her family is fairly new to upper middle class. Father an orthopedic surgeon in Rosemary-sur-Thyme, first professional following a line of tradesmen. Prefers work to his family. Mother is a city official's daughter, head of the Begonia Club and major benefactress to the Home for Spastics. Oldest child, a son, died in the flu epidemic. Rather a wastrel to that point. A young son is off at a public school."

"What about her?" I prodded.

"Hold on. Like you suspected the next was a girl, her older sister. A live wire type, cheeky blonde, Millicent. She weaseled herself into the fringes of society and snagged the second son of a something or other. He's become a famous architect. Don't much like his stuff, flimsy shim-sham Tudor with interiors like hospital rooms, but he makes the papers. Why he was even interviewed last week in—"

"Blast it, I don't give a damn about the brother-in-law. Get on with it."

He scanned the report. "Our subject of inquiry was late in life, grew up rather solitary. Sent off to a boarding school, very athletics conscious. She seems to have done well in classes and student activities, like the drama society where she worked backstage. Socially she was quiet and had very few friends, which explains her handling props and costumes in the dark."

"This all fits," I agreed.

"After graduation she wanted to be away from her family. A school friend's uncle was Lord Pfflugghh, that eccentric collector. That's how she ended up working for him. Her assignment was to attend auctions and jumble sales and add to his collection of match boxes, boots, and shrunken heads."

"Wait—then she would know how estates function, the service and the events," I interjected. "Why does she behave so cluelessly?"

"He paid her a salary. His collection was kept in a building in the nearby village, which is where she lived in between travels. Three years later she left, much to his displeasure, and rather disappeared—until recently."

"That's easy to explain, she worked for that agency as a companion."

"I'm afraid it isn't that simple. There's over five years to account for."

'How can that be? She's barely twenty-one."

"No," corrected Freddie. "That's what held us up for so long. She lied about her age on her passport and used her mother's maiden name."

"I can't absorb this. She seems so unfinished. Where was she all that time? Hasn't her family worried?

"That's the odd part. They not only know she's married to Algie, they even showed off photos she has sent to them."

"And the gap, her disappearance?"

"They attributed her behavior to the 'way girls behave these days,' independent. I don't think they missed her or thought much about her ever. Their detachment could explain her chronic self-abasement. It was clear they favored Millicent, who brought them into what goes for society in that godforsaken spot."

"Yet what would pull her from a plum position searching match boxes?"

"I've wondered about that. Secret pregnancy? No evidence. I think possibly a nervous breakdown, a hospital stay, and later work with the agency."

"Rather amazing, Freddie. Thank you, it all fits. Oh, I'm late for my house duties. Wasn't that just Letty's car heading to the manor?"

While I mounted my bike, Freddie cried out, "Isn't there something else you want to know?"

"What's that?

"Her name, you dolt."

"Ah, yes, what is it?" I shouted.

When he answered, I cannot adequately convey the tremor that tickled my spine with those mellifluously significant and signifying words. *Prunilla Crisp.* I floated away.

My Lady Consents

Just to confuse you, my dear reader, our Cesilly now becomes Prunilla from this point. I must say the reference to "prunes," a demure dried plum, added to guffaws once the staff learned the truth. I on the other hand thought of the original fruit's sweet flavor and aroma.

Some days later I entered the main saloon to face an unexpected commotion between Algernon and Mrs. Anvil. They were in one another's faces and pink with fury.

"I know he was here. Don't lie to me. Mr. Grubsnickle called me at the club last night to discuss a hunt, and mentioned seeing Philip's roadster about last week."

"It is Elmsby family business, no concern of yours. He did not want to come here, and he will not return. He's a reformed man, come to settle old debts and injuries. He needed my advice, that's all."

"Couldn't he have phoned?"

"I've known him for years. Aren't I entitled to a private face-to-face? You know I couldn't have gone to him." She dropped sobbing into a chair. "You know my promise to *her*. And yours to her as well before the wedding."

Algie bent down. "There, there now. I remember your pledge never to leave Slanderley until—"

"Until the rest of her returns. I'd die of worry wandering off and knowing an elbow might roll upon the beach with only Sloth to find it. He'd toss it aside."

"Forgive me, I have been so preoccupied with other troubles. You are right, Mrs. Anvil. But not further visits here from Mr. Elmsby. *Promise me!*"

She sniffled, "My business with him is done. You've nothing to fret in his account."

She left the room, while Algie waved me over. "Wait, Quirk, I haven't released you." At that point Cesilly-Prunilla peeped her head in.

"What a delightful surprise, dearest. I thought you wouldn't arrive until late this evening."

"Pressing matters urged my taking the earlier train. I hear Letitia took you to see Great Aunt Nan. Is she still here?"

"No, she said something about an event in Slurmouth."

I spoke up. "Excuse me, sir, but I believe Lady Horsham is attending a lecture by Swami Karmunivarti of the Society for Astral Enlightenment."

"Right as always, Quirk. That's why I like you around during tea and dinner conversations. What mistakes might we make were it not for you?"

Prunilla flashed twin dimples at me in appreciation. I'd never noticed them before.

"Your Great Aunt is so charming," she noted. "I think she must be very happy at Chilsworth. She missed you, however. Perhaps we can both go over again soon."

He grasped her hand, likely delighted she did not suggest Nan move back, then quickly dropped it and sighed. "I am very tired from travel. Just a light meal later in my room, Quirk. See you at breakfast, darling."

We were alone! I wanted to call her by her name, but was fearful to do so. "Pardon my curiosity, my lady, but I was wondering. About Great Aunt Nan—"

"My little fib? Algernon is so troubled of late, almost in the state when I met him. I did not want him to know of her failing mind. Her hysteria is obviously sign of an impending stroke. Letitia explained it all on the ride back. Isn't it sweet of Aglernon to keep her in such splendid care?"

I held my tongue. I didn't reveal that Nan's abode, however opulent, hardly supplanted Slanderley, in whose rooms she was born, schooled, wed, and wished to die. A futile dream.

Several weeks later my fears for Prunilla were set to rest. Philip never reappeared. Mrs. Anvil rampaged against Willets, the presumed source of the garter snakes in her underwear drawer. Algie's new bitch gave forth a fine litter. Letty presented him a tiger rug for his trophy room. "Let's just say the Swami has an extra-legal import business on the side," she told me. The sun behaved as though it might give our coastline more than a nodding acquaintance.

What follies our optimistic cells feed upon! This was the calm before the storm, the smooth channel heading to the Scylla and Charybdis, the fake truce in battle, Dr. Jekyll getting drunk before turning into Mr. Hyde. Well, you get the idea.

One Sunday a flow of visitors arrived for the day. Much to my surprise, Prunilla wore a new frock, new to us, that is. It had been worn before, an outmoded apricot silk from the prior decade. Still, it suited her and brightened her face. She even smiled, held out her hand, and attempted small talk. Later I learned Lettie was responsible for these changes. Prunilla was now an obedient puppet.

A group gathered in lawn chairs around her and Algie. During a lull in the conversation, Mrs. Scumbuttle whinnied, "And when shall the ball be?"

"The *ball?*" wondered Prunilla, as though she knew nothing about it.

"The fancy costume ball held at Slanderley for over a century. You must revive it. I thought the Bishop's wife already suggested it to you."

To my surprise, Algie interrupted. "I cannot not consider the return of such event. It brings back too many sad memories." He glared rapiers.

Mrs. Scumbuttle persisted. "Oh, but it would so make the season. We have been such a loss for fun in Slyme Gurney since lovely Ravina's departure. She would so want us to continue. Isn't that so, Mr. Wickleworm? Do add a word of support."

Being as love-starved as I of late, Freddie saw a chance for his selfish use from a houseful of guests. "Yes, I do agree, my lord. We need colored lanterns and costumes overflowing the rooms again. The house has been so empty of late. And a chance to invite those land speculators here. When they see our spread, they will cut us in their plan. Mrs. Scuttlebutt, I must ask your husband to join our little investment club."

Freddie's impeccable tact could be translated, "Hang Ravina already, Algie. Let's get those double-dealing syndicated people here and give them the shaft."

Algernon understood and took the bait. He apologized to Mrs. Scuttlebutt. She turned and snorted to her brow-beaten husband, "See, dear, I knew he would love my idea. Now you must take me to London to find the perfect costume. You can wear your usual armour."

Turning toward Prunilla, she mewed, "It must be in your honor, Lady de Loverly. As a new bride, you deserve a celebration. Algernon, how naughty of you not to have shown her off already. It was bad enough of you to deprive us of your wedding."

She leaned in closer toward the cowering hostess. "My dear, you must come as Bo-Peep. It suits your girlish figure. Too bad it isn't lambing season so you could tie one with ribbons to accompany you. Oh, perhaps you could put woolies on Lucy and powder her face white in disguise."

Tittering over her poor suggestion, she smacked her palm into the remaining cake. It took all my control to keep from pushing her face into it, and Prunilla's grimace implied she felt the same.

"I don't know about Bo-Peep but the idea of a ball is wonderful," she lied. What's this? She was learning the social graces, the art of smooth deception. "Yet I am at a loss for never having arranged one before."

Algie patted her hand. "No trouble. Freddie and Quirk handle all the details. As for yourself, pay close attention to Mrs. Anvil's advice with regard to your role. She knew everything about Ravina's contributions."

Prunilla actually blushed, stood up, and excused herself while she took a short walk. Freddie did the same shortly thereafter. He later reported to me his conversation with her, held in the pyramid folly. Essentially he reassured her that all would go well, just as the afternoon had turned out. When he chided her preference for isolation, she gave a curious response. "I do others a favor by keeping my distance. I can't explain why. Just trust me."

I congratulated him for developing his relationship with her and pushing her along. His endeavor freed me from spending much time alone with her and more in surveillance to watch for potential danger.

That evening Algie paced the floors of his trophy room, crunching tiger paws while tapping his pipe excitedly in his palm to punctuate his thoughts. "I know this is a big job for you, Quirk, now that the guest list is likely to be larger than in the old days—all those financial people Freddie wants to include. If you think it would be too much—"

He was fishing for an excuse to cancel, but I didn't bite. This was Prunilla's chance to show her new mettle, squelch her nerves and inhibitions. What ugly duckling wouldn't grab the offer to become a swan, what scullery maid a Cinderella, what weed an iris?

"No trouble at all, milord. May I take on some temporaries for the nonce?"

Hiding his disappointment, he mumbled, "Check with Freddie first on the expense. Must keep a watchful eye, you know. It is hard times, and we don't want to show off too much, even though we can afford to."

"Quite so. And will you require a costume this year? Perhaps break with tradition?"

"Of course not! Is it not enough that I open up my house as though it were an amusement arcade for hire?"

"I was thinking of something dashing to surprise people. Recall your father's motto, 'Always keep them guessing.' A toreador would make you stand out and show off your powerful calves."

"A Spaniard? Have you gone mad?"

"How about portraying great-great Uncle Albert, the non-lover of the Abbess at Tewksford-upon-Withie? We've a chest of his frocks. There's a majestic hunter green mandarin silk dressing gown. It would bring out your fiery hair."

"Why, Quirk, are you so determined to get my bile up? First you mention a Papist follower, then allude to the family curse. Hasn't it harmed me enough already?"

"I was thinking that wearing such robes would be an exorcism of the bad spirit. Don't you see? Show everyone you are no longer under its spell?"

"Let me think about that one. I'm very confused."

Lest you think me a nasty tease, I rush to defend myself. I had read of late a psychology book preaching the need for a strong self-image. Despite his inbred arrogance, Algie lacked in that quality. My proposal to toss over the family superstition was to build him up to be a proper husband to Prunilla, to absorb in full his role as stately Lord of the Manor. In other words, get an heir already. This hope was further affirmation of my pledges to Lord Leo and Ravina, to convert Algernon back to the playful boy singing off-key while he swung beneath a tree. It was part of my love for Prunilla, which I convinced myself was Christian *agape*, protection of all creatures of the kingdom, the sow bug and the sow.

Three hours later Algie stirred in his chair, my standing feet numb from the wait. "I think your notion is worth serious thought, Quirk. There must be a way to end the curse."

Preparations for the ball skated by with ease. Freddie oversaw invitations and finances, Mrs. Anvil the housecleaning, I the décor and orchestra. The latter proved the one vexatious task. The rage group, George "Birdie" Chesborough's combo, was booked. That left two curious choices: the flashy brass of Chippie Glugsberry, whose cacophony specialized in playing all tunes a quarter-note flat, little concern to the sweating, wriggling dancers, or the sinuous sounds of Veronica Nettlenose and her All-Girl Strings and Brass, whose earnest, musically accurate, and unremittingly boring style was favored by the horsey set, who drowned out the monotonous tunes with monotonous chatter of boots, jumps, and the price of oats.

Freddie and I flipped a coin to decide. It landed on edge in a chink on the floor, a precise expression of our feelings.

There followed several worrisome days. Birdie's agent then called to say the miraculous had happened, that he could make our engagement. It seems Birdie was holding out for a larger food bag, and hearing rumors we were considering Chippie, his once lead sarrusaphone, we somehow forced his hand. We gratefully accepted and paid less than we'd have paid the others.

The decorations were easier. In previous years Ravina transformed the halls into a Moorish seraglio complete with eunuchs, a tropical rain forest with free-flying parrots and toucans (one repeatedly dive-bombing the ostrich plumes in the head of the Bishop's wife), and an Egyptian temple dedicated to deLoverlyhotemtakhen VIII. My favorite was her Ode to Comedy of Errors. Its sets of twins became quintuples and octuples. With everyone wearing masks, the event produced errors well beyond Shakespeare's imagination. More than one person went home with the wrong twin, and not always to his or her discomfort.

Letty produced the theme for this year's decor, All-White, a reference to the (still?) virginal bride. This choice led to my ordering massive amounts of ivory China silks, Belgian lace, pearls, hothouse lilies, swans, bunny rabbits, and marshmallows. Mrs. Viscous planned a meal to include chicken breast in cream cheese sauce, cauliflower, white carrots, and potatoes, all arranged to disappear on bone china. Deserts were variations of sponge cake with white frosting, coconut, and rice.

Choosing a costume challenged everyone. Asking people to come in all-white would greatly limit the choices to white-tie-and-tails for the men, brides, bakers, scientists in lab coats, and a few uniformed occupations. On the invitations we specified "Come as You Wish." The implicit message was to wear something from the past, and save the effort of a new costume. Or go ahead and try to outdo your upstart neighbor with a custom designed bejeweled extravaganza. The men would appreciate the former, the women the latter.

In turn we agreed all family members would stick to the original theme. Prunilla fell into her boring self-abnegation. She was seen mumbling about, "What shall I be? What shall I be? A nurse? No, not fancy enough. Venus de Milo? What would I do with my arms? A lab technician? Too stern. A ballet swan queen? Not with these legs. Maybe Bo-Peep after all." A futile attempt to powder both Glocky and Lucy into lambs sent her slumped on a terrace lounge chair in a stupor.

One day Freddie called full of excitement. "She's got a plan, at last. Said she found the perfect idea and ordered the costume from London, the place Ravina used. Mrs. Anvil directed her there. She's actually going to leave us for a few days to get measured. She's not a bad looker when she tries. Rather cute dimples, though most of the time she keeps them hidden."

"Fabulous news, Freddie. Our hard work is finally coming to fruition. This may be just what the couple need to unite, and Slanderley may be rid of its curse. Now why do you chortle?

"That wasn't me. I thought you were clearing your throat."

"Someone's on the line. Mrs. Anvil? Are you snooping again?"

A sharp click pronounced her reply. That was the sole note of foreboding during the entire preparations.

On the day of the event, the bright sun surrounded frolics of fluffy clouds. I was grateful for the balmy weather, for Birdie cancelled out the day before. Someone snitched that he was being underpaid. Fortunately Veronica's band was playing in Plymouth. I caught her between shows and was relieved to learn she would cancel her next night there. I had to pay her a triple fee and arrange rooms for her musicians to use after the ball.

Her girls' initial appearance the next afternoon led me to hypothesize that music is the escape for the plain, the willow-thin, the overstuffed, and the long of jaw. Yet while directing their unloading, I realized they were spunky and sharp-witted. Veronica's real name was Betty, the desultory manner a charade. "We know those blokes won't listen to us," snapped a plump, gum-chewing harpist, "so why shouldn't we turn it down a bit. You should hear us when we play for our chums. A difference of day and night, Mr. Quirk." The little wink in her eye was as good as a passkey.

"I'll be by when all is over if you need anything special," I burred. "Something warm before you go to sleep perhaps?"

"Sounds right nice to me. My poor fingers and other things get so stiff after all that playing." Running a finger down beneath my chest, she continued, "They need a special massage, and you look like just the man for it."

At that I dashed behind some potted palms to calm down. Freddie joined me there.

"Why are you hiding? Plan to relieve yourself in the plant like a waiter at a posh restaurant?"

"Just coming down from an enchanted encounter with a woman of talented fingers. I have lost any prejudice against lady musicians. My evening is set."

"Why do you think I was angry Chippie backed out? His boys' real music goes on after hours when I invite them to my place."

"For your sake, Freddie, I hope one of your land syndicate guests shares your preferences."

"I'm not hopeful. Say, is Algie costuming?

"He's in his boudoir discussing the matter with Lucy, who's snoring in her usual spot. I cleaned old Lord Bruce's white satin bathrobe just in case, but I doubt he'll cave in. He'll stick to his formals, pretend he is playing a Lord of the Manor. At least Mrs. Anvil is in high spirits and is much nicer to Prunilla these days. Algie is kinder as well."

"The other day he told Prunilla a husband was akin to a father and must protect his wife from unhappiness, nourish her innocence. She agreed she would rather accept his counsel because she had such a hard time making decisions. It's a curious bond, but seems to be settling in."

"Of course—their own *modus vivendi*. Each couple must decide. Guinevere and Launcelot? Trilby and Svengali? Castor and Pollux?" Freddie rolled his eyes to cut me off.

"And who are our pair then? Mr. Barrett and his daughter, the hypochondriac poetess?"

'You still doubt Prunilla?"

"Five years unaccounted for. Isn't that enough?"

We were interrupted by another pert member of Veronica's band. She flashed her opaline eyes at me to bleat, "Have you got a plunger?"

"A what?"

"A plunger, a plumber's friend."

"Is there a problem with the loo?"

"No, silly, it's for my horn. I use it to doo-wah."

"I'm sorry, I don't understand."

"She held her trumpet up and pointed to its bowl. "See, I unscrew the rubber cup from its handle, stick it in here, and wiggle her in and out. Doo-wah, doo-way."

"Ah, a mute," I replied, wondering whether she too had hopes for after the ball.

"You're a quick one, you are. We lost our bag of plungers on the train, new ones too. The last hotel we was at had bad plumbing. You can wash them afterward, but they never lose the smell. Betty got them just for this show."

"Did you notify the train authorities? Perhaps they were left in the car."

"Naw, I'm sure the albino sharing our compartment took off with them when he left at Slickthistle Epsom."

"I'll see that they are replaced. I'm sure they are available in Slyme Gurney."

"Just so they don't stink. Nothing worse than smelly doo-wah."

La Grande Débacle

As the hour for the ball approached, I went to assist Algernon. As expected he vetoed the costume, yet agreed to a sprig of Lily of the Valley, a display he'd have rejected in the past. He flushed with anticipation, a young settler about to meet his mail-order bride. "What shall she be, Quirk? A goddess, a scientist, a swan queen? Or a winsome Bo-Peep? I hope not the last. Lucy's ears are too short."

"The doors are about to open, your lordship. Shall we go to the hall? I believe Mrs. Anvil has arranged a late appearance of her ladyship once the guests have arrived."

The hall was soon a cage of odd ungainly creatures. The Bishop's wife, a butterfly in chiffons, seemed more a rainbow stoat. His Sacredness bore a monk's robe of brown silk instead of sackcloth. The usual array of cats, whose furry wired tails threatened others' eyes as they bounced about. Three "Pinky" reproductions of various height and girth, along with one "Blue Boy" well beyond youth. Two Arab potentates laughed with a belly dancer (Alice Glub, the bane of her Methodist parents). Two halves of a horse danced together, surrounded by jesters, pirates, and a smattering of milk maids. Letty and Reginald loomed over with matching white-suites and top hats. Too bad they couldn't dance.

Following the first set, I announced Prunilla. I cued Veronica, who directed a dirge processional at top volume to quiet the guests. I gently pointed them to the top of the staircase, from which the radiant hostess would descend. Algie fussed with his shirt cuffs as he craned upward.

Prunilla glowed while she drifted down the stairs. Letty gasped. Algie's face drained. Pausing near the bottom, she extended her hand out, "My lord."

"What in God's name is this?" he cried.

"The lady in white from the portrait upstairs. Charlotte!"

"The slut and suicide? You dare mock me?" He pulled her close and sneered, "Go and change immediately." She ran off in tears.

Turning with a smile, he pronounced, "My friends, please ignore this minor indiscretion. Wipe it from your minds. She was unaware of the last person to wear that costume. My wife will return shortly. I accept all blame for this break of mood. Music, please!"

I glimpsed Mrs. Anvil atop the stairs, haughty and triumphant, the perpetrator of Prunilla's gaffe. Dashing up, I growled, "You wretch. You did more than send her to London. You told her what to request. Why?"

"I mentioned the likelihood of famous portraitures, the inevitable Pinkies, the Lady in White. I only suggested she examined the family portraits for a possible idea. Can I help that she fell in love with Charlotte's gown?"

"Small chance. You know Ravina wore the same dress. I'm sure you made up some story of how Charlotte was loved in the Slanderley's past."

"What if I did? Had she a grain of spunk, she'd have a costume of her own choice from the start. Will she ever learn to think for herself?"

The ball was far from ruined. Hungering gossips had much to chew, while more discrete ones played generous to Prunilla when she reappeared in a black crepe suit befitting a social worker.

Letty found me to say she smoothed things over with Algie by suggesting Ravina misunderstood which painting to copy. "But she is broken-hearted by his reaction. She did so want to get a rise from him."

"You can't believe they are still unconsummated, Letty. It's been a year."

"Which reminds me, when do I lose my virginity, Eddie? Don't you like the drape of my trousers over my finely sculptured hips? Wouldn't you like to slip off my shirt studs, reach your hand into my puffy breasts?" She pushed me behind another potted tree and pressed my fingers on her glorious left mound. I was fairly delirious, ready to submit.

"Hullo, you two. I see you." Reginald peered in. "Playing a little game of hide-and-seek? I win."

"Yes, dear. Quirk is repairing a broken stud on my shirt. Isn't that sweet of him?"

"Good man. Carry on. I'll be in the card room, Letitia. So trying, this dress-up stuff. Must save my energy for a morning ride. If you ever want to leave Slanderley, Quirk, we've a place for you. Would pay much more than Algernon."

By now Letitia was moving my hand elsewhere. I could scarcely stammer a thank-you to Reginald, who scampered away unconcerned. Since in his mind our petting could never exist, it never would, even in his full sight.

A glimpse of the harpist brought me to my senses. Letitia was my half-sister—time to break the news to her before our passions ruled. Tomorrow, I swore, I would find a moment.

Gently untangling myself, I led her around the plant toward the card room. Passing a full-length mirror, I glimpsed how alike we were in profile. My handsome profile was a dramatic one in a woman. Only my smaller chin and lighter coloring prevented a full giveaway. That sight furthered my determination to confess. Our desire for one another was merely Narcissus's wish for union with himself. It was time we were released.

After the ball, the trumpeter proved a virtuoso, such that we planned to meet in Penzance in several weeks. I was free the following day, and began it with a breakfast at Aunt Jemima's. She was curious to learn all about the brouhaha at the ball, word having already reached her.

"It was such a pitiful sight to see her ladyship so dismayed by the silence, then humiliated by Algernon. She did indeed look beautiful in that gown, and the initial gasps were over how stunning she appeared."

Jemima said, "Of course Algie reacted that way. No one could match Ravina with her elegant slouch. She'd make prison scrubs reek of glamour. She spent hours before the mirror setting poses. Still, it was all pretend, that one. No inner beauty. Just chemicals and playacting."

"How can you be so bitter, Auntie? Did she ever harm you? Do you know of anyone she hurt on purpose?"

"Yes, Algernon. Having watched him grow up, he is like a nephew to me. He was a sweet child, but his mother was crazy, and you know where his father's real interests lie. It's no wonder he lost his verve. Just because he is dull and narrow is no reason to dislike him. He means well. Consider how he protected the creature following her cruel gaffe last night. You say he even danced with her. As for Ravina, he was as good a husband as could be."

"Now it is you who spins stories, Auntie. You don't know the truth behind Ravina marrying him."

"Did she tell you some tale of woe? Don't expect me to believe that, my boy. She knew how to play you, just as she did any man. You continue to daydream rather than take women as they really are. I hear you have lost Rose, such a shame. Why can't you be loyal to one woman?"

"Blasted—why is everyone quick to criticize my bachelor ways? Really, Auntie, I don't want to hear another word on either topic. Now excuse me. I'm out for a walk."

Striding away I was so angry I tripped in a rut, ripping a hole in my trousers, gashing my left knee. My palms had shreds of skin with little stones embedded within. The stinging felt almost good, a sign I was more than just the mental vapors people accused me of.

A heavy fog hung about the roadway, causing a yellow roadster to swerve around me and spin into a stop. Out leapt Philip Elmsby, the last person I expected. I wasn't aware he was back in the area. Mrs. Anvil had suggested he would not return to Cornwall.

"Old man, I hope I didn't hurt you. This blasted weather calls for X-rays to see what's ahead. Let me drop you at the pub so you can wash down there."

"I'm fine, Philip. I tripped on the road before you passed by. But I could use a drink."

"Just a quick one. I have to catch a plane." When we settled there, he began, "Heard a rumor about some nastiness at the ball last night. Is it true Algernon berated his wife in public?"

"It's more complicated than that. Someone suggested her ladyship wear Charlotte's gown, similar to the one Ravina wore at her first ball. Algie took her choice as provocative, to unsettle him, and he reacted accordingly."

When Philip inquired who could be so devious in making that suggestion, I was on the spot. I chose evasion.

"At first I thought it was Mrs. Anvil and even fought with her afterward. Later I overheard another guest titter about misleading her ladyship and realized she was the perpetrator. One of Slyme Gurney's noted troublemakers. I must find a bauble of remorse to present to Mrs. Anvil later."

He seemed to accept my account, and bragged about his sheep ranch, his exceptional success and membership in the best Sydney private club. I deflected him from discovering that I knew of his nefarious partnership with the housekeeper.

After waving Philip off, I bought some butterscotch for my nemesis and returned to Slanderley. When I couldn't find her, I suspected she was up in Ravina's room and slipped into the side chamber with the peep hole. Prunilla was there, shaking.

Mrs. Anvil was midstream, "…all the men made love to her, so beautiful her ways. His lordship adored her. You should never have married him." She pointed to a pastel portrait of Ravina. "You'll never take her place. You're so pathetic. The only ones who love you are Lucy and Brambles, both too senile to notice you aren't *her*. Fit for old dogs, that's all you are good for."

Prunilla crossed her arms over her chest, sobbing. The old crone suddenly shushed and held out her hands. "Here, I mean no harm. I want you to accept the truth, do what's best for Algie, for all of us. Do you really think you belong here?"

"More than you," stammered Prunilla while drawing back toward the large windows. "You have hated me from my arrival, done all you could to force me out, even turned my loving husband against me. You won't face the truth that without Ravina you are nothing."

Mrs. Anvil shoved Prunilla back against the open ledge. "Ravina? Poor armless child asleep in the church yard. That's where you belong, don't you think so? Look back down behind you. See the rocks? They welcome you. They are reaching up for you. It will be over in an instant. Jump!"

I burst in at this point, but both froze, as soon did I. A deafening horn blared from the sea beyond, following by the sound of exploding rockets.

"What is it?" cried Prunilla.

Mrs. Anvil blanched, then fell to the floor, crying "It's the sea. It's taken another."

A Mystery Solved

Taking advantage of Mrs. Anvil's collapse, Prunilla rushed out, knocking down a boudoir chair and tripping to the floor. I extended a hand of support, but she stared at me accusingly. "Oh, so you're a partner in crime too, Quirk. Don't think I am ignorant of your plots." She pulled herself up and dashed downstairs.

What did she mean? Had other threats been made to her? Did someone lie and say I was against her? Had she caught Sloth following her and suspected I was behind his spying? Whatever, her reaction was troubling, for it meant she mistrusted one person she could depend upon.

Mrs. Anvil remained slumped on the floor, a pitiful sight, eliciting no charitable impulse from me. It was all I could do to pick her up and shove her out the open window to the rocks below.

I found Prunilla in the main saloon, where Kenneth was telling her that Algie had gone down to the beach. Unaware of my whereabouts, he said I was there as well, which normally would have been the case."

"You say you were with Quirk."

"Yes, milady. We were gabbing in the servants' hall."

"Seems like Mr. Quirk can be two places at once," she sniggered. "Do you all get great fun out of lying to me?"

"I don't understand," puzzled Kenneth.

"I think you do. But don't worry. I shan't be here much longer. Then you will have Slanderley all to yourselves again. Now get my coat and a thermos of tea to take to his lordship. Don't stare like that. Go now!" So equipped, she passed through the terrace to the beach path.

Meanwhile I rushed another way to the cliff overlook. Below village folk arrived from different directions to gape at the scene in the water. A ragtaggle fleet of row boats moved through misty air toward a small commercial ship sitting aground on a reef beyond Slanderley Cove. A lifeboat was pulling off, while a tug waited for tide to return so it could move in and free the vessel easily. Since no one seemed to be injured, a festive air suffused the onlookers.

Heading down, I located Freddie in the crowd and asked where Algie was. "He pulled off a lifesaving. Seems he was among the first here, and saw a ship crew member leap into the water, where he injured himself on the reef. When Algie heard him screaming for help, he swam out and pulled him to an arriving motor boat. They took the bloke by sea to the nearest sanctuary station to fix him up."

Really? Algie hates the beach and water, I thought. Who knows what can instill courage? Even in Algie?

"I'm not surprised. Algie has so few opportunities to prove his mettle," I suggested. I think the last time was during Barney's auto accident. He tried to patch him up and stayed with him while he died. Then he arranged a trust for the invalided sister."

"He was surprisingly splendid then." Freddie agreed. Where were you anyway, so slow in getting down here?"

I described how Mrs. Anvil almost killed Prunilla, and how the latter then accused me of malignant plans.

"Did she really tell you to leave her alone? How marvelous that she piped up for herself."

"I only wanted to help her, and am confused by her anger," I complained.

"Look, old chap, you do hover over much. Perhaps it was your constant supervision that has her wondering about your real intentions. Part of maturing her is to let her feel freer to be on her own. She is an adult." Then he tipped his hat and departed.

That "old" was not an adjective to warm my ears, now tickled by hints of grey. The fog slinked out beyond the listing ship, creating a sunny steam cabinet atmosphere. Gulls swooped overhead, gawking and squawking in parody of the people below. As I clambered up toward the manor, one bird left his opinion oozing over my balding pate.

I was about to enter the main saloon when I noticed Prunilla speaking with a stranger in some uniform. I held back in the entrance, unnoticed.

"So you see, Captain, we have no knowledge of my husband's whereabouts, and I fear I can be of no use to you. Could you return perhaps at five? His lordship is a man of habit, and I know he will be here then."

"My lady, you would do me a great favor to convey my message directly to him as it is of a most sensitive nature. Please sit down, this is disturbing news. We sent a diver down to check on the reefed ship's hull to ensure there was no serious damage. While poking about the reef, he discovered a small sailboat, fully intact, with the name *Le Ris Prochain*."

"Ravina's."

"Yes, the very one."

"But I thought it was all broken up in an accident somehow. At least that was the theory."

"So we all believed. The diver says it rests like a child's toy in the bottom of a tub, in one piece."

"How very odd." She stood and began to pace about.

"But there's more. He went further in, where he found a body. Its features are all melted by now, just a skeleton really, but it is there for certain."

Prunilla gasped in concert with me. A body! Who could it be? Had Ravina taken a guest? A lover from the city somehow not linked with her? Was Aunt Jemima's salacious theory correct? But no one other than Philip was heard passing by, and he is alive. How to make sense of the corpse?

Algie came in through the terrace. "Oh, Captain Seaspray, I regret I wasn't here upon your arrival."

The Captain repeated his story. "We are most regretful to revive painful memories, and shall endeavor to keep our findings as quiet as possible. You appreciate, however, that now I must report the body to authorities so an identification can be established."

"Of course, Captain. Do all that is necessary. You have my full cooperation in the matter."

I pretended to arrive from somewhere else and escorted the man out. Then I went to the terrace, where the doors remained open to let ocean breezes flutter through. Perched behind a shrub out of their sight, I could pretend to be keeping guard were they to discover me.

"I'm so sorry, dear. You must pack and leave immediately. He spoke as to a child. "I suggest someplace in the North where no one will know you and you can reestablish yourself with full use of the estate funds."

"I understand. I have been a terrible wife, and deserve your eviction, especially given how I dressed at the ball. I really didn't know--."

"You, no, it is not you. I do love you. It is Ravina in the boat, come back to haunt me. I mean to protect you."

"But you identified her body. As did Freddie."

"What there was of a body! No doubt some poor soul who committed suicide off a cliff, the right sex and size. I said it was Ravina, the return of the Slanderley curse."

"But why send me away? It's natural to mistake a longtime drowning victim. And I love you, I don't want to leave you."

"You can return in time, but I fear we are soon to be separated for good. You see I shot Ravina, and the world will now know. I must pay the price."

"My dearest," swooned Prunilla. "How awful to have borne that secret. You truly must love me to confess to me!

And to think I took your cool attitude to mean I was no match for her."

"I apologize for my distance. I needed to test you, to know you were not a slut. When the only man you had eyes for was Freddie, I began to sense your genuine loyalty. And when I saw you last night in Charlotte's gown, forgive me, I knew you did mean to draw me in closer. I was harsh as a charade to the shocked guests. I knew you were mine alone, and planned for us to return soon to Monte Carlo and start over."

"Oh, my sweet love," shined Prunilla. "You do love me, you do. We must flee this cursed place. I'd heard about the Abbess's threat, and now it has come true again."

There followed sounds of sucking and sighing. I was too shocked to move. Algie's confession was beyond my expectations, yet Prunilla's worship of a murderer suggested depths of masochism Dr. Freud himself could not untangle.

Prunilla spoke up. "Sweets, does anyone else know?"

"Not a person who could even guess."

I had a sudden urge to sneeze, my conscience no doubt, but stifled it.

"There's still a chance nothing will come of it. The Captain says the body is much destroyed."

"You're right! You see, I shot her in the cottage. The bullet passed through. There may be no sign of her wound."

"To think all this time I thought you still loved her. We may be free after all." (More sucking noises) "Why did you kill her anyway?"

"She forced me into marrying her! During her first Slanderley ball as a guest she teased me insufferably. At a party months later she tricked me into taking her home. On the way, it's very humiliating to admit, she forced herself on me. Later she said she was pregnant, not true of course. She said she'd tell all that I had raped her. As a gentleman I had to do my duty. She changed her manner at that point and said she would prove to be a valued wife and hostess. Instead she turned the place into a brothel for her own delight. Her wickedness is too despicable for your innocent ears. I know you must have heard stories—they're all true."

Prunilla peeped up, "Actually, everyone has gone out of their way to praise her. Freddie, Mrs. Anvil, Sloth, the maids. Even you, my dearest, which confused me. Their constant admiration forced me into ever more despondency."

"Just more of Ravina's chicanery and deception. If I praised her or mentioned her, it was unwitting. I wager every single one of the others was indebted to her, psychologically or emotionally. They're all quick to pretend how generous she was when she likely blackmailed or bought each out. I was the only decent person in the household. Even my devoted Quirk was in her control. I had to act, and make it appear an accident." I could hear him move closer to the terrace doorway and slinked down more, grateful for the darkening dusk.

"The chosen evening I feigned a headache and had Quirk lock me in my boudoir. What no one knows, apart from previous occupants, is the secret staircase from the dressing closet to the trophy room. I took a pistol I kept there, crept to the cottage, shot her while she was combing her hair. Funny, she looked so surprised when she noticed me in the mirror. I carried the body to the boat, rowed to the deepest side of the reef, opened some seacocks and stayed until the craft sank. Then I swam back to clean up the cabin and went to bed. When a body washed ashore later, I took advantage of the situation. I felt safe, that I had pulled a perfect crime. I so hated pretending to mourn that I took off to Monte Carlo."

"What if they discover the truth now?"

"I am prepared. I will make the others admit to her treachery. I will claim I was doing a favor by removing her evil. Unfortunately there is no mercy for mercy killers."

"Oh, Algernon, come here again. You have *me* forever. Even if a trial occurs, we shall find you an escape. I am a clever girl, and it is my turn to confess. I pressed Mrs. Cribbage to introduce us at that yacht party. When I watched you stare up at the stars so meaningfully, the thin mourning band on your sleeve, I was compelled to care for you. Even though you were far above my place, I spun myself a fairy tale, and made it come true. But with you I am also a moral person, and in time felt guilty for my trickery. Hence my anxiety and nervousness. I feared you would turn on me for using you."

"But what poor girl in your place would not?" he replied. More kissing followed.

Lord, what a melodrama was unfolding. I could not bear to hear more, and crept off

Further Twists

And what now was my moral responsibility? To report Algie or not? I chose not. The law was due soon to come in. Anyway, I had testified at the original inquest how I locked Algie in his room early that night, before Ravina returned from London and went to the beach cottage. Having provided his alibi, would they believe me now?

There remained the possibility that Prunilla remained in danger from Mrs. Anvil. Just who was good and who was evil in this overcomplicated story? I must move very carefully in response.

When I entered the service dining room, Sloth was enjoying some cider. Looking up to direct me to about the sounds through the windows from above, he remarked, "Sounds like an animal caught in a trap. I must go and check it, put it out of its misery." His Cheshire grin followed.

"You needn't bother. It's just a conjugal mating, long neglected. Speaking of which, how has your little spying of Prunilla progressed. With all the ball preparations, we've had no time to discuss your latest findings."

"I do just what you say, and keep out of sight. There's little to report. She took to walking to town several times, the back way over the treeless fields, so I couldn't follow her but once, on a misty day. She bought some chocolates and went to the druggist, though came out with no package. Then she went to the public phone behind the market."

"That's all? You never saw her with anyone? Think hard, Sloth. There's a bottle of best brandy for you, two even."

He wrinkled his brow like a mastiff. "Now that you mention it, I do recall Philip was in the chocolate shop. Of course I couldn't hear anything, but I watched them a good five minutes. They wasn't too friendly from her face. I couldn't see his face but his ears were glowing."

Later on I carried the phone to Algie, a call from Colonel Mustard. Naturally I listened in from another receiver.

"So the body I identified must have been someone else. The few strands of hair convinced me. The sight still gives me nightmares," he said.

"I understand. I only needed your word for the record. It is thus all the more difficult for me to ask."

"That I identify the body in the boat? No, I'll be relieved in a way. That poor girl who lost her arms. Now Ravina can rest in her proper place."

"Suppose I pick you up tomorrow about nine? The boat should be beached by then. Inspector Tittybath will accompany us for the record. No need to consider the matter further."

I hung up gently, to be taken aback by the reflection of Mrs. Anvil in the mirror before me. "So who's spying now," she hissed. "His lordship will not take well to his favorite servant eavesdropping. It's about Ravina, isn't it? Don't lie, or I'll go and snitch."

"I have no intention of prevaricating, my dear lady. I am worn down by plots and mysteries. Yes, she is in the boat."

"Free at last! She is home! I am here for her proper internment. God has graced me with more than I deserve."

"I am pleased to agree. Enjoy while you can, Mrs. Anvil. Your days here are numbered. One day you shall slip up and a witness will share my testimony."

"My soul is also free, Mr. Quirk. No one can harm me again. As for leaving Slanderley, that day is none too soon. I long to fly away. Once my business is finished, you'll have no more bother from me."

Now it was time to take Freddie into my confidence. I found him at his cottage and free to hear me. He was equally surprised by my account of the couple's bizarre conversation.

"This is too worrisome. Now we have real reason to fear for Prunilla," he expressed, "and not from cocky Philip and deranged Mrs. Anvil."

"I don't follow. Who would hurt her now?"

"Algie, of course. Now that she knows, he has reason to do her in. Look how cold-blooded he was in killing Ravina. His lovemaking to Prunilla was a ruse. Things will go on smoothly if he avoids the law, which I fully expect. Then one day Prunilla will meet an accident."

"So we must hope the law succeeds, and do all we can to see it does."

"But if it doesn't, Eddie, it will be your word against his. Either that or we sway Prunilla to our side, which appear hopeless now. I doubt we can trick him into a more public confession. I don't like any of the options. We do enjoy our lives here, don't we?" He said that with a look to indicate "We've never heard of murder, have we?"

Passing over the bridge of Charlotte's fall, a shuffling noise swooped by my ears. Something moist ran down my neck. An owl's talon had struck, scarring me with its wisdom.

Identification of the body went as expected. Colonel Mustard, Inspector Tittybath, and Algie returned to Slanderley afterward for a late lunch. Given the casual chat of weather and local gossip, I surmised any evidence of a bullet wound was swept away by the sea currents.

Later I received the local paper, headline: RAVINA DE LOVERLY'S BODY DISCOVERED, WHO LIES IN HER GRAVE? I chose to use it to plant doubt in Prunilla's mind about Algie, to make her see the madness of and ultimate danger in her position.

Handing the paper over to her, I remarked, "It's so sad for all of us, milady. The staff wishes to relay our condolences over this shock."

"Thank you, Quirk. I do appreciate all the good thoughts."

I turned to leave, then looked back, as though having another thought. "It was so surprising for us, her being the consummate sailor. It's curious about the disaster. Mr. Sloth was out in the early morning, a fit of insomnia, and mentioned how calm it was. He said the wind would not overturn a child's sail boat. Well, it has been over a year, and his memory is likely rusty."

"That is often the case with Sloth. I take no notice of any of his remarks. He's a horrid man, always sneaking up on me."

"Well, no matter. If it ever came to court, the weather men can be called up to testify, can't they?"

"Court? Whatever for? It's all been settled."

"Forgive me, milady. I'm repeating village gossip with no regard to your feelings.'

Her hands clasped in worry. "What do they say? I'd rather know."

"To be frank, all along people believed Ravina died at the hands of someone. People in her, and your position do inspire envy. Or some mad person, perhaps." I made an artful pause, "in our midst."

"Now you are being reprehensible. How dare you speak to me that way when my husband suffers so grievously!"

"Again, milady, I only repeat others' talk to suggest we need to stop all the wagging tongues."

"I see your point, Quirk, but leave me now to think over this." She flipped her hand away, a new gesture of command.

Later I passed by Mrs. Anvil's rooms. I noticed her packing clothes and belongings into travel boxes.

"You are leaving us, Mrs. Anvil?"

"Yes, though I don't know the hour yet. I merely wish to be prepared. If you are here to chastise me, then say your words and be off."

"Not at all. My concern is for your health, the shock of recent events. You have by all accounts continued your usual exemplary way with staff. I simply wanted to suggest you take a holiday."

"Isn't it strange, Mr. Quirk, how grief draws out kindness? Please leave me be. But before you go, I have one piece of advice. You'd do well to start packing yourself."

"I shall miss your efficiency, but my praise goes no further. I leave on no note of false flattery. As for your advice, I am bound to Slanderley until eternity."

The next day brought the Coroner's Inquest. Freddie and I sat in the back of the hall with the villagers. Mrs. Anvil arrived with Philip. Widgeon chauffeured Algie and Prunilla, though she remained in an ante hall until late in the testimony.

The first witness was the doctor who first examined the body. His gruesome details brought gasps of fright. He attributed the death to drowning. The police on the scene commented the same.

It was not until the boat builder, a burly Welshman, took the chair that the truth as I knew it eventually began to emerge. "She were a most seaworthy vessel, having once been a small fishing boat in Mallorca. A solid sailor's mate. Lady de Loverly had the knack. I should know, I took her on her maiden trip with it. Anyway, I was out that night myself. The winds were just enough for pleasant sail under the moon. Nothing difficult to handle."

"But what if Mrs. de Loverly entered the cabin for sustenance. Could a sudden gust topple the craft?"

"Not at all. It wasn't built so poorly. I take umbrage at your suggestion."

"I apologize. I only mean to track all possibilities. How then do you explain the sinking?"

"That takes no expert. The police called me to verify their impressions. The seacock to the drain was open and a small spike hole in the hull, not visible until I looked close in. The boat sank on purpose, by human hands." The crowd burst into clamor.

"Quiet, please! Do explain for the unfamiliar the role of the seacocks."

"They are part of the plumbing fixtures, like the drains. They are closed before leaving port, otherwise the incoming sea water would sink the ship."

"Thank you for your expert voice. Lord de Loverly, will you now let us hear from you about that evening?"

Algie walked solemnly to the appointed place, serene, hardly the sight of a murderer about to be exposed. My heart beat faster. Were he the murderer, even out of madness, he must pay the price. He must be revealed to prevent his harming anyone else, Prunilla most obviously.

I turned to the back of the room to see her slip into the last row. She was pale, her eyes glassy. A lost soul, yet one who could be saved, I hoped. I refused to believe she truly supported Algie being a killer. Other women had sat in a similar place, others would follow. Typically the mothers and wives of criminals deny the malignity of their men until convinced otherwise. Prunilla's support in light of Algie's confession to her was perverse.

I shook myself visibly to attend to the testimony.

"So you have no idea how a spike hole occurred, or that the seacock remained open?"

"Of course not. I hadn't even been down to the beach in some time. It was Ravina's to oversee, not my charge."

"Who tended the boat for her?"

"When necessary she called upon its maker, Mr. Peasbottom, who just enlightened us. I believe he returned the boat a few days before the accident."

"I see. Well, we'll return to that later. In your opinion, could a trespasser have entered the beach unnoticed"

"Highly unlikely. The staff living in cottages on the estate are likely to hear. We also have a couple of guard dogs let out at night. They would alert us to any stranger."

"Then, milord, you are intimating the boat must have been tampered with by someone on the estate itself."

"Logic suggests so," he replied.

"It pains me to ask you this, sir, but did you and the late Mrs. de Loverly have a happy marriage? Had you any unusual difficulties?"

"I dare say if you asked those who knew us well, you will find they report us content. We were married many years, and accommodated one another's needs well."

"Oh!" swooned Prunilla as she fell to the floor in a faint. Was it the shock of his lying?"

"Would someone please assist my wife," Algie directed. When the commotion ended, Prunilla carried out of the room, the coroner continued his questioning.

"Was there anyone else at Slanderley who could have taken ill-will toward the deceased?"

"No, none at all. My staff, under the guidance of Mr. Quirk and Mrs. Anvil, are all loyal and devoted, not to add by nature kindly souls. I should ask that I be suspected of foul play before any of these individuals."

"We most assuredly wish no such intimation. Your own attentiveness to your wife's needs, your abundant generosity, are all matter of record. That leaves us with an insoluble problem as to who tampered with the boat."

"Not if you consider the obvious person?"

"And who is that?"

Aware of the drama of the moment, Algie casually examined his fingers while replying, "Why, Ravina, of course."

Once the coroner hushed the clamor, he pursued the questioning further. Algie wove certain facts into a portrait of an unfulfilled woman, childless, whose increasing distress pushed her toward despondency. No longer did her charitable works make up for her barrenness. It was a moving contrivance, making Ravina a saint whose frustration pressed her to choose death. Royal Academy players would be hard pressed to surpass his performance.

The jury deliberated scarcely a half hour. They returned the verdict "death by suicide."

Blackmail

Outside, villagers surrounded Algie with words of consolation. I noticed Mrs. Anvil and Philip by the Priapus fountain arguing about something. They stopped once they saw me. It was then I recalled both Aunt Jemima and Freddie had heard or seen Philip's car the night of Ravina's death. Where did he fit in the events of the evening? Had he seen Algie at the beach? If so, why was he silent? Of course—his appearance could make him a convenient suspect.

Freddie stopped me to enlist my aid in arranging the burial of Ravina, to take place late that afternoon. Algie wanted to put everything behind him and see her in her proper place. We avoided discussing the inquest and went through our paces like condemned men. We each wondered whether our tenure at Slanderley must end.

The private services were spare and elegant, to Algie's taste, not Ravina's. She'd have wanted a brass band and grand party afterward. Prunilla stayed away. Philip sat in deep grief behind a pillar. During prayers my mind wandered in turmoil. Algie was my half-brother, and I had sworn oaths to both his father and first wife to protect him. How could I arrange an "accident" to remove him? Yet he confessed to be a murderer. All I could do was hope evidence would arise to force justice.

Afterward I discovered Philip had let himself in to find Prunilla in the saloon. "Isn't it almost dinner time? Aren't you going to invite me to stay and join you at the table?" I wanted to wring his neck, though Prunilla seemed unperturbed.

"Mr. Elmsby, I am very tired following the day's events, and so shall be Algernon. We do welcome you to visit tomorrow. For now, do us a kindness and leave."

"Think I'm a lout, don't you? Not at all. I admire you though, the way you've pulled off this caper, come to Slanderley and enjoy all the benefits so much due to Ravina. It is *her* house and always will be. The place was little more than a scruffy hunting lodge before then. It's truly admirable the way you don't give a whit for anyone except Algernon, and even that's all show, isn't it?"

He moved closer to her, while she held her hand up toward me to keep out of the way. "You needn't be afraid of me—we're cut from the same mold," he sneered. "You're just a hanger-on, a tiny sucker fish feasting of a fat lazy fiend so stupid he thinks you are doing him a favor. I'm here to suggest a little proposition. Think how much further we could go in concert."

Unable to watch any further, I dashed to get Algie, and found him hugging Brambles in the trophy room. "Elmsby is drunk and pawing her ladyship," was all I need say. Freddie dashed with him to the saloon as well.

"What in God's good name is going on here?"

"Hullo, Algernon, your Most Glorious Lord. That was a most commendable performance at the inquest."

"Quirk, see this brute out, and none too gently."

"Hold on! I think you better hear me out. Let's stop pretending. Do stay too, Mr. Wickleworm. Do you not execute Algernon's most private plans? I doubt any of this will surprise you." He went to Algie's favorite chair, sat down, and leisurely lit a cigarette.

He continued, "Let's get right to the point. We know the suicide verdict was wrong. You, Algie, had me fooled until the disclosure of the open seacock and spike hole today. The others protect you to preserve their leechlike existence." He made sure to look at each one of us.

Algie sat, crossed his legs, and gave a look of unconcerned poise. "The coroner was meticulous in his interrogation. If the verdict satisfied all else present, villagers and experts alike, why not you, Philip?"

"Suicide? Would a suicide write a note like this?" He waved a sheet of Ravina's stationery. "No, it stays in my hands. She sent this to my hotel." I read over his shoulder while he spoke:

Dear Philip,

I have very important news to share. I'm off to Slanderley today, so if you get this in time please come down as well. I'll sleep in the beach cottage tonight, and will leave it unlocked so you can enter quietly.

R

We all gasped. What was she planning?

He continued, "It was my blasted luck to be drawn into an important event and not get her message until the next morning. I called down to learn she was missing. Anyway, I left for Australia assuming she would be found. Mrs. Anvil has kept me informed since then. Now what if I had given the coroner this note today? Doesn't look too good does it? Rich man's wife inviting the old beau to visit privately? Makes a good case for jealous rage if the husband knows."

"Give it to him then," Algie answered while waving his hand away.

"We all have our price," continued Philip. I'm sure you can see to that, old boy. I don't think you want the new bride to be known as the widower of a wife-murderer."

Freddie jumped in. "Do so Algernon. You can afford it. Don't let this rogue destroy your life." I realized Freddie said that as a snare. If Algie accepted the offer, he as much as confessed to all of us that he killed Ravina.

The ruse failed. Algie directed me to hand him the phone. "Colonel Mustard? Algernon de Loverly here. I don't know how to say this, but some fascinating new information has come up concerning Ravina's death. It is urgent you come here without delay."

I served drinks while everyone sat in silence. Philip's greed seemed true to form, though I could not understand his profiting from Ravina's murderer. Prunilla downed two strong gins, most unusual of her. Freddie and I shared glances of frustration. We imagined Algie in the defendant box to hear the sentence, "Guilty in the murder of his devoted wife."

Kenneth led in Colonel Mustard, red-faced and muttering, "Right at the start of dinner. This better be worth the interruption."

"Colonel, my good friend, Mr. Elmsby, in full light of all of us here has suggested a preposterous blackmail scheme, all on the basis of a vague note Ravina sent him the day before she disappeared. Show it, Philip."

Mustard put on his glasses and spent a long time with the message. "Interesting, but it doesn't lead us anywhere new."

"What do you mean?" charged Philip. "It is proof Algie is the murderer. Don't you see? He's been insanely suspicious for years, thinking Ravina and I were lovers."

"This hardly leads to your conclusion," noted the Colonel. You have lived in Australia, with a few brief returns. How would he even know she asked you to visit that night? This message could be seen as the need to convey some last wish. This won't do at all, Mr. Elmsby. The case is closed."

"Oh, I get it. You can't go up against the local aristocrat, can you? You eat at his table and your wife's charities benefit from his largesse, while I'm the well-known rogue, though that is no longer true."

"Put down that drink and go home," advised the Colonel. You're drunk. Algernon could not be guilty or he'd have taken your blackmail offer."

"No I will not leave! He lied about his happy marriage. I heard how often Ravina was away from the estate, and slept often in her cottage."

"We all know the lordship's sad accident years ago left him disinclined to motor or even travel much. He is a devoted country man and understood Ravina had her London activities. We all knew her from childhood as mercurial and full of wanderlust. He married her in full knowledge as well."

Turning to Algie, the Colonel added, "I have never told you this, but I always admired your appreciation that she was like a headstrong horse needing to run free at times."

"I appreciate your kindness, and apologize for disturbing your evening," added Algie with a broad smile.

As the Colonel turned to leave, Philip dashed to the door and slammed it shut. "Now you hear me out. What about Sloth? We know his tendency to wander about at night. I want him questioned."

In the ensuing discussion, Algie convinced the magistrate of the need to remain and settle the matter. He rang down for Sloth to appear, while I crossed my fingers. The man entered a veritable Quasimodo. I thought he overdid the idiot bit when he bent down and drooled to Prunilla, "T'other one was prettier."

Colonel Mustard reviewed the purpose of the discussion. "Let's talk about the night Ravina died."

"The lady lost in the boat?

"Let me handle this," interjected Philip. "It's my claim."

"Do you remember me, Sloth? Long ago I used to visit her at the beach house. We invited you for cake some evenings."

"Never seen you. Who is this?" He peered quizzically around the room for help and continued his refusal to know anything.

Philip flustered, "Of course you remember me. I know how you liked to poke about the beach late at night."

Sloth bent his face into Philip's. "Never seen 'im before."

Philip tried to turn the conversation to the evening Ravina died, but Sloth's foolish act blocked his efforts.

Mustard flustered. "I'm through, Philip. This fool wouldn't remember whether he ate breakfast this morning. With your allowance, Lord Algernon, I leave too."

Algie held up his hand. "It's my turn now. Have patience and we'll soon get to the end of this. If Ravina invited you Philip, how do we know that you that you weren't here that night, that you murdered her?"

Foiled Again

Freddie squirmed during Algie's accusation toward Philip. Had Algie seen Elmsby's car the night of the event and could turn the story around?

Philip reached into his pocket and brought a news clipping out of his wallet. "Here is a social column that refers to my presence at a party that evening. As you will note, several MPs were there, and I've no doubt will corroborate my presence. My best witness, the wife of a noted shadow cabinet member, can verify my presence in a certain Kensington flat later that night, if you so wish to inquire."

"Looks like we're at a draw," commented the Colonel.

"One last proof, it is my right," added Philp. "Quirk, will you please ring for Mrs. Anvil?"

I could barely contain myself. Here I was rooting for the very people I had feared these many past weeks. Whatever trap they set for Algie, I doubted he would wriggle out. Prunilla cowered in her chair. I hoped I would now have the opportunity to report her knowledge to the authorities and see her as well in a gaol cell.

Mrs. Anvil entered in regal style. Though dressed in all black, she wore a pair of Ravina's ebony earrings. The Colonel began.

"Good evening Mrs. Anvil. I trust you'll excuse our interruption. We have important questions to ask concerning Ravina's last days. I should like to begin by inquiring if you know of the relation between Philip and Ravina."

"They were cousins by adoption."

"That is all? No hint of additional connection."

"If you mean were they lovers, no. That bizarre belief is spread by some fools in the village, but they have no basis in fact. Those two were more like sister and brother, able to confide in one another."

Algernon's right arm began to rise as though to strike at her, then quickly brought it in control to make it seem he was tugging at his shirtsleeve. The Colonel continued, "Could you detail what you recall of her activities that last day, Mrs. Anvil?"

"Not by direct knowledge, I'm sorry to say. Letitia's staff had come down with the flu, so I answered her call to help out several days. With Ravina was in London, I was not needed here. Regrettably I went to the Horshams and never saw her again. Perhaps she would have slept in the house were I here to assist her. I could have brought her cocoa with my special herbs to help her sleep."

"A sad loss, Mrs. Anvil, my condolences. But what about her schedule? You must know her usual activities, here and in London."

"I suspected such was the point of your call and have with me her diary, left in the morning room desk before she went to the city. She was very organized and kept careful records so

I would always know where to reach her. Here, read the page for yourself." He took the gilded carmine leather book and began:

"Brown Hotel.

10 am, Breakfast with Aurora.

Noon, Hair salon.

2 pm: Snit, B 6219.

4:15: Train back.

Snit? Who is that? Do any of you recognize a Snit?"

Algie suggested it was obviously someone she was to visit. He interpreted the note as referring to a B phone exchange in London and gave me the duty of locating the source through the phone information service. Kenneth refilled glasses while everyone avoided one another's eyes.

I brought a phone extension into the saloon so all could overhear. Biggengotham 6219 responded with a child of perhaps three who thought me his grandfather and dove into a long discussion about a "Wooster" named "Authuh." Cutting off my call, I tried Bumberry 6219 to be yelled at by a crotchety Mr. Snickers Magog, who shouted about always getting wrong numbers.

My attempt at Bliss 6219 brought minor success. It was a medical office, answered by a night porter. "There was a surgery here that closed very unexpectedly. Though t'were a successful practice, he were a very young man to retire. We thought he fell into an inheritance. He were a lady's specialist, a Mr. Snit. Sorry I can't give you any more information."

I put the Colonel on the line, who used all his grumpy authority to achieve a home address. The doctor had moved to a posh area in the Cotswolds.

"Well, there's little we can do tonight," said Algie. "I suggest we compose a letter and request an appointment to see him."

"No doing," Philip shouted. "Who's to say a second letter won't follow? Or that someone might not creep out to visit him in the meantime? I insist we head up together the first thing in the morning."

"I'm inclined to agree," seconded the Colonel. "We must arrive unexpected to view how the witness responds spontaneously. Do you think there's a link between Ravina's message and her visit to the doctor? I suppose so given it was sent to Philip late in the day."

"That is why I think this is so important," Philip explained. "Hasn't it occurred to any of you what kind of news would follow the visit to a lady's physician? Algie, have you considered that you murdered your own heir along with your wife?"

"Get him out of here before I—"

"Murder me too? Tsk, tsk, such violence from a gentleman. So you know I make no foolishness in the meantime, I hope Freddie can accommodate me overnight at his place. But I also wish a guarantee of no escape from *his* part," he added while nodding at Algie. "We all must be watched."

Recomposed, Algie coolly ordered, "Mrs. Anvil, after Mr. Elmsby leaves, accompany me and my wife to my boudoir, which you are to lock from the outside and leave as such until morning. Does that satisfy, Philip, or do you expect me to have wings secreted under my shirt?"

With a sweeping bow, Philip gave a mocking *au revoir* and left, adding, "I'll fix the fire, Freddie, while Kenneth accompanies me to assure I do nothing to foil the plan. Then you can fill me in on everything said after my departure."

Colonel Mustard wiped his damp face. "Oh, what an obstreperous lad. So sorry about this, my lord. I fear that the collapse of his claim may lead to his notifying dailies later with nasty lies. I suggest you two take a long vacation until these latest events blow over. Leave it to me to squelch any rumors."

"Thank you, Colonel. I knew I could depend upon you. Quirk will see you out, while I consult with Freddie."

Freddie later came to my room. "It's the oddest situation. I don't get what's happening. Algie is as cool as an ice sculpture. After Mustard left, he looked at me sadly and thanked me for all my assistance. He seemed almost a weepy basset hound, saying the wonderful days were over for him. Prunilla cut him off. She explained he was still overwrought from the shock of the body, and led him to bed, followed by Mrs. Anvil.

"What do we do now, Freddie? There's that secret staircase. They could still escape."

"I forgot about that. He might have been misleading us through his performance, by hinting Philip would be proven correct. We both know Philip is just guessing, while you still lack witness to what you heard. You were outside, so it would be easy to challenge you in court. Prunilla would back him too. You are in a dangerous spot, Eddie."

"We are, you mean." "

"No, you are the only one to hear the confession. If they find out you know, well. "On that incomplete remark, Freddie held up his palms in helplessness, turned, and left.

Any doubts about Prunilla soon evaporated. I answered a call for her from Letitia and listened in.

"Dear, how sorry we were to miss the inquest. The results are horrible. Can't you get Algernon to do something?"

"Why, Letitia, what can you ever mean? The jury was quick and unanimous with the verdict."

"Of *suicide*! What a disgrace to the family, and Ravina's memory as well. She could never have done such. Had she aged into a crone, she'd have clung to every last second. We must get the verdict changed. Suggest a traveler or a Communist murdered her. I've a good mind to call some people myself."

"Suggest murder to avoid the shame of suicide? Really, Letty, you are going too, too far. Please wait on this. We are heading to the Cotswolds tomorrow, a trip that should clear everything up for you. Now do be a good sister-in-law and get some rest. And no calls to anyone in the meantime."

"No worry. I just remembered there's a sheep sale in Fenlickshurst-under-Wren tomorrow."

Dear Letitia, innocently fanning the fire. There'd be little rest for the partners-in-crime tonight.

The next morning the Colonel joined haggard-looking Algie and Prunilla in the town car, driven by a new chauffeur, Squamous. Because they did not trust him to rush ahead and influence Snit in some way, they picked Philip up on the way out.

Left behind, the hours passed like molasses. I couldn't visit Freddie because he called to say he had an unexpected trip to London, some crisis over a land deal in Prussia. Feeling sorry for myself, I wandered down to a beach shrouded in spectral fog. For the first time in years I rolled up my pant legs and waded in the cool ripples.

"Aye, Mr. Quirk. How be ye?"

"Very tired, Sloth. And you?"

"How'd you like my performance last night?"

"What do you mean?"

"My dumb act."

"You mean you lied to us?"

"Where the coin lays, my tongue will follow."

"You're saying Lord de Loverly bribed you. You saw him that night at Ravina's place."

"No, I didn't see him, though I saw someone. I didn't tell him that though."

"What do you mean?"

"The night Ravina died I was out about midnight and saw someone get into a yellow car hidden in the grove closes to the beach cottage."

"So Philip was here after all. But that's impossible."

"No, t'weren't him. I couldn't see well, just a rough silhouette. The person were definitely smaller than Philip. Wore a cape, which he'd never do, and a funny peaked cap."

"So you think this was the killer."

"Not exactly. I didn't go near the cottage. The whisky got to me and I went off to bed. His lordship knew I went out late at night 'cause I had seen him take off in early hours for some secret meetings. He were giving me money regularly to keep quiet. Even so I am bound to defend him in any circumstance. He's never done me wrong, just the opposite."

"Still, you could have told the truth about the yellow car."

"If the authorities ever come up with it, I'll step forward. Otherwise me lips are sealed. Best not to stir up the bees when they're not stinging. What if the caped visitor didn't harm her? I'd only be stirring up trouble for some innocent person. Anyways, the verdict were suicide, and that's my bet."

"I warn you Sloth, on my mother's memory, I may one day press you to come forward."

"Fair enough, Mr. Quirk," though I doubt I'll never need to give such."

Revenge at Last

During the afternoon Kenneth advised me that Mrs. Anvil was packing all her goods into cartons to send ahead to the train station. I went to her sitting room, now stripped of its doilies, photographs, and vases. She was wrapping a large bowl in paper.

"Do you wish to give your notice, Mrs. Anvil? Are we to lose your celestial tones and graceful figure?"

"Beastly man to the end," she growled. "I give no notice to you because I do not know yet the time of departure."

The phone rang, causing both of us to startle. Kenneth answered and buzzed us. "It's for you from Colonel Mustard." I took the line with hands atremor, hopeful and fearful at the same time.

"I thought I'd pass on the good news. The lord and lady have gone to spend the night at a hotel. I'm staying also after dining with friends. We had an awful row with Philip after visiting Dr. Snit, but the case is definitely closed now. Lord de Loverly was tremendously relieved and discussed a visit to Spain once the inquest papers are sealed tomorrow. So you may save time by preparing their trunks in the meantime."

"Thank you, Colonel, for the advice. I would also be most grateful if you could possibly divulge the results of the conference with the surgeon."

"Not at all. He was most obliging. Offered the best single malt while he searched his files. He explained he was long Ravina's regular surgeon for female needs. She was concerned about not becoming pregnant and consulted him toward that eventuality. He discussed various treatments he tried over the years, unsuccessful unfortunately. Great chap, invited me to dine at his club next week."

"Ahem, the last visit?"

"Ah, harrumph, yes. He showed us his notes. Ravina had a malignancy and would die within several months. Before then she would be bed ridden and on morphia. He said he explained all this and she took the news without upset. A jolly girl, he said, not given to upsetting display of tears. Well, I had to say that was cause for suicide."

Hearing this account, I felt struck down with an axe. If Algernon got away with murder this time, then he had reason to murder Prunilla as well. He'd return from Spain a widower. The vision of her smashed at the bottom of a mountain ravine clutched my heart. I'd lost my affection for her, but not my concern for her safety.

When I put the phone down, Mrs. Anvil asked for the findings. I just shook my head and left. I knew Philip would be on the line soon with his account. Better she learn from him, someone sympathetic. Very likely her departure would join his, possibly with him to Australia. They must leave Slanderley for their own safety as well.

I stumbled in the dark to Freddie's place. His phone was separate from the mansion so I could call him in London away from the eavesdropping of Mrs. Anvil. My attempts were futile. He was not at his private club nor the flat he kept there. Meanwhile I concocted reasons to keep Algie from taking off quickly for Spain. I fell asleep there, hoping Freddie would get one of the messages I left and ring me awake.

What roused me was not the phone, but the pounding of horses' hooves and neighing in the distance. Widgeon must have forgotten to hook the stable latches after his evening check.

Then shouts from further beyond reached my ears, sounds not of horse seeking, but of alarm. When I opened the door to hear better, I glimpsed in the region of the house a frightful sight, orange-told embers dancing in the sky, a witch's bonfire. Slanderley!

Gathering my boots and courage, I dashed up the path to find to my relief only the stable and garage were ablaze. The surrounding trees and grounds were wet from rains, which was beneficial to the fire brigade. Yet if the wind shifted directions, as it tended to do on nights like this one, it could whirl flames over the closest wing of the house. When I arrived, the men were handling hoses and ladders, while the women ran buckets to the spot fires nearing the house.

"What happened?" I yelled. "How did it start?" Someone handed me a heavy coat for protection while I changed into my work boots.

"*She* deliberately set it." I followed the nod of the man speaking to a point to my left. Mrs. Anvil stood in a stupor by the rhododendron wall. "She was just about to spray gasoline on the wing when I caught her. I smacked her hard, so she's in a daze. No need to fear. Always knew she'd do something crazy one day."

She stood immobile, murmuring under her breath. Turning, I paced evenly toward the troubled lady to appear unthreatening. I spoke calmly. "Mrs. Anvil, you look cold. You'll get sick after all the damp from the rain. May I help you? Wouldn't you feel better inside?"

Her eyes widened a bit as she seemed to recognize me. "Please, sir. Take me away. Fire frightens me so, reminds me of an accident long ago. All that horrible flame crawling over skin, chewing at it." She fell into a slump.

I half-carried her into the house and into a side chamber used for storing chairs. She sat in one and asked for some brandy to calm her nerves. I placed a rug upon her for comfort and headed out to get her drink. Before I reached the door I heard a loud snap.

"Turn around, or you're bound to join Ravina sooner than you would like." She held a small pistol from Algie's collection. "It's loaded. You know he always keeps them ready. Now go out ahead of me, back to the barn."

I had no choice. Indeed my prospects appeared better there, in the company of my fellow workers. She poked me outside again, then stopped, barrel pushed into my back, while she watched the flames. A sound mixing cackle and delight startled my ears. The others were too harried to notice my predicament.

She continued to mumble while my heart banged away, certain my minutes alive were numbered. It made sense she wanted to destroy Slanderley, where she'd known so much unhappiness. Had Philip called her and told her Ravina must have committed suicide after all? What drove her over the edge?

Suddenly she spoke aloud to me. "You thought you knew everything, you with your spying ways. You could never imagine the truth, nor did you ever want to. I was just a convenient enemy and scapegoat to you. But it was all so obvious if you only opened your eyes and looked."

I felt the barrel push harder, expected to be shot, but instead fell to the ground. Mrs. Anvil had shoved me aside and was now running toward the flames.

"She was my daughter," she cried. "Ravina was my daughter."

Punctuating her cries was the sound of metal crashing through wood and onto rock. From the sounds I could tell it was a car over Charlotte's bridge. Ignoring Mrs. Anvil and the fire, I turned to rush straight through the copse, branches tearing at my face.

I ran in terror toward the sight. Was it a villager speeding the short cut to help stench the fire? Or Freddie back from a drunken bash in London? It was the worst sight of all.

I shall never erase from my memory the colors, odors, and textures of that abominable scene, the obscene silence accompanying it. The bridge was broken through, the lights of the crushed auto illuminating the devastation. Sprawled on the rocks on her back was Prunilla, eyes glazed open in surprise, a thin stream of blood flowing from her side into the cool stream. From under the wreckage of the submerged car, waving at me with help of the current. was the left arm of Algernon.

Fool Me Once

The caprice of the world sometimes votes on the side of justice. Prunilla survived, paralyzed from the chest down. I was among the first visitors allowed to see her. She appeared in the bed a small child, so sweet and vulnerable I could not help but lean down and kiss her cheek.

"My deepest regrets, I began in feigned sympathy for the loss of her husband. "I expect it must be hard to know that in some tiny way one contributed to the death of another. Such a dreadful accident. Was it the commotion of the fire? The moonless night?"

"You don't have to pretend any longer, Quirk."

"What do you mean?"

"Why don't I get to the point to conserve my energy? I killed him. I crashed us on purpose."

"What are you saying?"

"It's true. He murdered Ravina just as he murdered my fiancé. Who knows how many he murdered before then?"

"I'm sorry. I don't understand."

"The auto accident years back. Ravina's good friend and decorator Barnaby was my lover. He was also the designer for the theatre company I acted in. They couldn't bear a daughter having such plans and made my life a misery throughout childhood for my love of music and dance. They fixed up a job with a lunatic match-box collecting aristocrat, hoping I would marry him. That only convinced me to run my own life."

She began to cough, so I helped her sit up and drink some water. "Don't exert yourself so," I urged.

"I must continue. One day I changed my name so they couldn't find me, moved in with a girl I met at drama class, and started over. It turned out I was a good actress, and found not leads of course, but small paying parts from the start. That's how I met Barnaby—he was the first person who had total faith in my future on the stage. We fell in love and planned to marry. We had dreams of becoming a famous theatre couple, his doing the backstage creative work to enhance my onstage performance. We were young and naïve, but did have the talent and drive to pull it off."

Her eyes glazed briefly in a death mask, then fluttered back. I began to worry for her health.

"Forgive me, this is difficult but necessary. I even came to Slanderley with him. Ravina's city friends were artsy types, and we were drawn into her circle. You wouldn't remember me because I had my natural auburn hair, very long, and wore clothes fitting my curves."

"I vaguely remember such a visitor, but your crowd was so noisy and incestuous. I couldn't be bothered when you were around. You insisted on taking care of your own drinks once I set up the carts. I was happy to get the afternoon free." Thoughts of afternoon trysts flashed in my mind.

"I adored Ravina," continued Prunilla. "She was eccentric and given to poses, but she was so tolerant of all kinds of people, even an aspiring actress. I think she even loved Algie in her own way, but I'm ahead of my story."

"Are you up to all this?"

"Yes, silly—or should I say Cesilly? I know all about that one too. My back's broken, not my vocal chords."

The matron interrupted. "Five minutes are up. Our patient needs her rest. Call tomorrow morning to see if you can visit. We mustn't strain ourselves, must we?"

Walking into the waiting room, I was surprised to find Philip pacing about. "Quirk, what are you doing here? They won't let me in to see her."

"What's this turnabout? A fine how-you-do after all your schemes. I overheard your plotting with Mrs. Anvil. You can't lie anymore."

"I beg of you, hear me out. Come for a spot of tea while I explain." He put his hand on my arm in appeasement, and though I pulled away, I sighed and agreed.

"Oh, all right! This had better not waste my time. I have to get back to Slanderley to arrange repairs from the smoke damage."

Once seated and served, Philip drew a wry smile that only angered me again. "I'm dreadfully sorry, old boy, to tell you you've been taken on a rather nasty frolic."

"Blast it, Philip. That's nothing new with you around."

"The point is, I've known Aurora, your Cesilly or Prunilla, for years. Ravina introduced us during one of my annual visits over. We met in London and she took me along to a theatre party. That's how I learned her real name and origins."

I connected the dots. "So Aurora was her stage name! And it's the name of the person Ravina had breakfast with on the day she died. She was more than just a passing acquaintance."

"That's correct. After Barnaby died, Ravina became like an older sister and consoled Prunilla. She made sure others in London kept her active and comforted. She even told Prunilla about the auditions for a European tour, one that helped her through her grief."

"She is still pained to talk about Barnaby. The nurse cut us off just as she was going to say more."

"They were a couple made in heaven, it was obvious to all. She swore on his death there'd never be another."

"Yet she married Algie, mooned about the place after him. Not to mention confess eternal love when—"

"When he admitted killing Ravina. We expected you'd be snooping then. But we are rushing ahead. The story needs its full unfolding."

I was dumbfounded. What did he mean "we expected" that I was snooping?

"I've been involved in a very different way, Eddie. When Ravina went to breakfast, she was excited over the possibility of being pregnant. You see, I was there with Prunilla as well, though she'd never put me down in her datebook for fear Algie would see it. She said she'd let us know after she'd seen Dr. Snit.

"She did send a message to me at my club, as you already know, asking me to meet her at the beach cottage that night. I mentioned it to Prunilla on the phone. Then I was called to join a rabble of politicians I needed to soften with regard to an upcoming investment. She teased me about a gossip item involving me with a Cabinet member's wife."

I laughed, because I knew the story.

"Worried about Ravina being alone late while waiting for me, Prunilla decided to go down herself. She called her understudy under pretext of family emergency, and borrowed a car from a fellow actor."

"One similar to yours."

"Only insofar as it was a yellow roadster. Hardly anything as stylish and distinctive as mine, but in the dark I suppose all yellow cars look alike to the unwashed."

"So she was the secret visitor Sloth noticed. What did she learn? Wait a minute. How stupid of me. You two have been in cahoots all along."

"What else could I have been saying? Just hold on. The point is Ravina learned she was definitely pregnant. She wanted us, her closest friends then, to be first to know. She hoped the news would bring Algie out of his isolation and despondency."

"So the next day you called down to learn she was missing."

"And when Prunilla came over to tell of her visit to the beach cottage, we were sure Ravina was fine. No pregnant woman would put herself in danger. She had waited so long for this blessing. I had to leave immediately for Australia, with the understanding Prunilla would update me on the situation. As weeks passed, we grew ever more worried of course."

"But how did you ever suspect him? What brought you both together in some kind of plot against him?"

"It was when the first body was found. Believing it was Ravina, we too connected the dots. Prunilla never accepted that Barnaby's death was an accident, though the police report was against her."

I remained confused. "Given she believed Algie responsible for Barnaby's death, why did she marry him?"

"Revenge can feed the most odious tasks. That's precisely the point, her realization he killed Barnaby." Checking his watch, he leapt up. "Sorry, I have an appointment. See you about this again soon, no doubt."

"Hold on! You can't leave me like this. What about Barnaby?"

As he rushed through the door, he tossed back to me, "Prunilla can explain."

Fools' Justice

Duties called me back to Slanderley, so my frustrations continued. I arranged specialists to clean to the damaged rooms and refurbish them by the time Prunilla was ready to return. I hoped to see her in a few days to hear the rest of her story. That evening I stopped in to review the day with Freddie.

"You suspected all along Algie had the stuff of murder in him. Why?"

"You're so naïve! I handled his business. He displayed a killer's instinct in his deals, no moral concerns at all. He wasn't above paying unseemly types to do nasty jobs for him, like dig up information for a double cross or bribe. As in Dr. Snit's case. He had me make out a large monthly check to that greedy codger. That's how he could retire in style so early. I suspect now that after Ravina's death was announced, Snit sent a letter of condolence referring to the unborn child. To cover his tracks early on, Algie made sure Ravina's medical record allowed no reason to doubt suicide. The doctor would have been a major slip-up."

"So you didn't know at the time?"

"It wasn't my place. I managed the books. He kept separate accounts for his black activities. I never asked, just as he never bothered me about missing funds following my trip to the races. We had an understanding. Why do you think he hired me?"

"You're suggesting Slanderley thrives off a stream of questionable activities."

"Yes, and to your benefit and all of ours on the estate. Some of the legal investments went into war industries, here and on the Continent. So don't be so sanctimonious. Most of it wasn't against the law, just more forward-looking in light of saber-rattling in Germany. Ravina certainly didn't mind the steady flow of riches for her useless artistic hobbies."

"What do you make of Prunilla's role?"

"A damned fine little actress. Too bad she'll never walk the boards again. You'll have to ask her directly. I really don't care. I'm too busy with the estate settlement.

"What is in the will?"

"The usual most-to-my-wife thing. Money to his private concerns, even some gifts for the village, a new bandstand in his honor and a refurbished hall for the theater group in Ravina's honor. It was written years ago. He told me he'd update it in a few months upon returning from Spain."

"When, we suspect, he'd return with no wife to favor anymore. I wonder whether they were onto each other's game to do one another in."

"They turned out to be a good match in a top level chess game, didn't they?"

Several days later I returned to the hospital, but was forbidden entry into Prunilla's room. Her family had descended like Greek mourners about to raid the widow's nest. Elder sister Millicent was lodging near the hospital to keep Prunilla company and guard the visitor list. She let everyone within hearing range know she was Lady de Loverly's sister, and demanded treatment accordingly. It was a long week before I could see Prunilla again, thanks to my consorting with nurses to require Millicent to sign some papers.

As soon as I entered, I was delighted to see her color back to full health. Foolishly, I blurted "Barnaby."

"Yes, more pieces to fill in. My first clue was when Algie came to the memorial service. He looked me sadly in the eyes and whispered he wished he had been behind the wheel, that he could have managed the curve. What struck me about that remark was Barnaby's previous mention of Algie's quick and accurate reflexes, which meant he had let him drive his cars in the past." A tear rolled down her face.

"The other clue was when I recalled how before the accident Algie watched Ravina and Barnaby embrace when he arrived. There followed the long discussion of the car and its potential. Algie dripped praises over it and begged for a long ride afterward. They scheduled for the next day. You know the rest."

"The accident."

"What appeared to be an accident. Grief drove me to view the official report. I needed to know exactly how Barnaby died. The wreckage was all on Barnaby's side. I wondered how a car supposedly out of control didn't smash head on into the wall. The inspector said they had gone through all the possibilities, that I was just upsetting myself. Yet I couldn't help thinking that Barnaby might have survived, that his unconscious body was shifted into the driver seat and his neck broken, the stated cause of death. I thought of a cinema short I had viewed, how really good drivers can create an accident to design. Horrible visions. I thought I was going crazy to follow that path."

"I understand. I have a way of spinning stories to the extreme. Sometimes I never know what truth is because I become so caught up in my imagination."

"Precisely. Being an actor, I readily shift into that confusing state. I have yet to always separate my stage role from my real life." We looked at one another in sympathy.

"So when Ravina died under strange circumstances."

"That's when I contacted Philip with my theory. He'd known Algie longer, and shared tales of his cruelty to animals in childhood. He was also a direct victim of Algie's black mail schemes, driven off to Australia as a result. He brought Mrs. Anvil into the discussions, and she told of Algie's growing black moods before Ravina died. She also found our conclusions concerning both deaths believable. She admitted she had come to similar doubts herself."

"Wait a minute. You, Philip, and Mrs. Anvil were in this together? But I saw you threatened by her several times."

"Hardly. She set the scheme when she informed us that Algie was heading to Monte Carlo. She filled me in on Algie's need for the opposite of Ravina, a frumpy and obsequious mouse. That set the snare. I hired another actress to play Mrs. Cribbage. We deserve awards for our performances. During the wooing I found just how adept Algie was behind the wheel of a roadster. Oh, the dead sheep! He hit them on purpose! Now I knew my theory was right." She shuddered her porcelain shoulders.

"Still you continued with your plan. You could have found a solution other than marrying him. I mean, that required considerable intimacy with a possible murderer."

Laughing, she replied, "I knew from Mrs. Anvil he did not have a normal sex drive. Anyway, it's not like I was a virgin. I was ready to be a Lady in bed, close my eyes and imagine the Glory of Britain."

"This is all so complicated. The staff was always around. How could you manage?"

"Once moved into Slanderley, Mrs. Anvil and I created vignettes to send you astray. You were a special danger because you were known to be a habitual snoop. And there was your filial devotion to Algie."

"How did you know that? It's a secret."

"She laughed almost to the point of choking. "Haven't you looked at your bodies? Your faces may differ, but your athletic builds and proportions are identical. You're balder and grayer now, but everyone in Slyme Gurney knew you were Algie's older half-brother. Even had you not resembled him, the story would have been out in little time. We couldn't take a chance with you knowing the truth."

"How very kind of you," I minced.

"That's not the only reason. We didn't want the staff to become attached to us as well. We were playing a deadly game and needed to keep everyone else innocent in case anything went awry. Fortunately our set-ups worked. I wish we were cleverer in our dealings with Algie. We had to play it by ear, and chose mental torture as our best strategy to break him down and confess. Your snooping did not help, and I was ever alert to listen into your phone calls to keep ahead of you."

"So you were the eavesdropper, not Mrs. Anvil."

"Yes, except for mid-afternoon hours she'd stay by the phone in Ravina's old room to cover when I was out."

"It seems your plan was not working."

"Not for a long time. Algie was unflappable. His stolidity got on our nerves. Philip and I had some rows in the village over our failure to unhinge him. We were sure my use of the Charlotte gown would pull the plug on Algie's sanity. Mrs. Anvil was losing faith as well. As much as she wanted her daughter's name cleared and death avenged, she could not bear living at Slanderley much longer. We didn't realize he was happy with the curious marriage, that the costume only drew him closer to me."

"Didn't it occur to you that one form of Algie's losing control would be to murder you?"

"Of course. It was a cat-and-mouse game, though he was unaware of such. Anyway, I expected you would be close by and avert his moves. If my death exposed the killer of Barnaby and Ravina, it would have been a fair sacrifice."

"You certainly fooled me. Freddie and I ran ragged trying to protect you from Mrs. Anvil and later Algie."

"From Algie? I don't understand when you came to that conclusion."

"I overheard his confession to you after he learned about the body in the boat. I knew then you were in danger for learning the truth from him."

"You heard? But I saw you leave the room."

"I slid out and around the house to lurk on the terrace behind the large urn near the open door."

"How terrible. Do you realize what this means? Oh, God, forgive me!"

One look at her face and I understood her despair, our despair. Had she known I witnessed his confession, she need never run the car off the bridge. Had I trusted her and told her of my knowledge, we could have moved forward together to see him charged. Unaware Prunilla was conspiring against Algie, I held my silence. I in effect turned the wheel of the car with her.

The Story Ends

The shock of our realization left us wordless in the hospital room for many minutes. So much of my behavior over the years depended upon my idealization of women. Ravina fulfilled that role well. I resisted fidelity with good ones like Rose because she was too real and earthbound. Early on I even idealized Prunilla, then tried to reshape her, and eventually despised her.

The others were correct: I arrived at middle-age with the emotional quotient of a child. By never exploring and moving beyond my childhood intentions, I stunted my growth. My false beliefs made me a killer, secondhand, yet responsible nonetheless. My oaths to my father and Ravina turned into a catacomb's dust.

I took Prunilla's hand. "We did what we could under the circumstances. In lying to one another for what we thought were good reasons, we set up a wall preventing truth to free us.'

"That's a harsh philosophy, Quirk, but a comforting one."

Upon later reflection I realized my father and Ravina had set up the impossible for me. Immature, I accepted their charge as a knight of old, imagined myself a hero. They were unfair in their knowledge of Algie's dark side. The burden would have crushed someone much more capable than I. I understood their wishes, and held no grudge. Being so capable in house service, I covered my many weaknesses.

Prunilla improved steadily as the doctors expected. On a later visit Philip sometimes joined in, so we three laughed over Cesilly, azaleas, mock threats from Mrs. Anvil, and clothes made drab on purpose. He made his final farewells to us, disclosing he was returning to Australia never to return. When I clasped his hand for the last time, I observed the gray at his temples, the wrinkles crackling his once-fine skin.

Another time I teased Prunilla about her unexpected wealth. "You can do whatever you want now, perhaps even learn to handle a chair and take to the stage again. There are many roles where your being able to walk are unnecessary."

"I don't deserve it, his money. I wasn't his real wife. Not even during that afternoon confession. Haven't you noticed Millicent and my family have not been around to annoy you of late? It took less than I expected to satisfy her."

A month after the accident I approached her door to find a sign, *ISOLATION: NO VISITORS*. The matron at the desk explained Prunilla had developed pneumonia, a serious problem for paralysis victims. This was a time before antibiotics. All the doctors could do was try to control the fever and hope she was strong enough to overcome the infection.

The next day I arrived to be told she had died around sunrise, without awakening. "It was as though she wanted to go," commented the surgeon. "She told me last week she had just finished all her work. She did not seem interested when we told her about rehabilitation. Still, for such a healthy woman."

The service was simple, with only estate staff, de Loverly relations, and her family, who shoved to the front whenever one spotted a press photographer. She was placed in the family crypt, well apart from Algie. When the mourners left, I hung a brass plaque in a dark corner. "God bless the anonymous sinner who lied to tell the truth."

In a promise to her family, I sent off the items she arrived at Slanderley with, some books and decorative pieces. I packed up her clothes, the newer ones, for the church jumble sale. I found the Charlotte dress in a box in the top of a closet and kept it for myself.

I also encountered Algie's most personal belongings for the first time in many years. His boudoir was fresh, waiting for him to arrive for sleep. In his changing chamber, I found the secret door with a narrow stair leading down to his trophy room.

Partway down the stairs I found another door that opened onto a long windowless hall. Within it were books and pamphlets relating to Germany and Hitler. A trove for his secret nighttime meetings? So he was among some aristocrats who preferred alignment with the Huns and other fascists. Some had been vilified in public, so the rest must have gone underground. What group better to appeal to his darker side? Compensate for his weak manliness through ritual and claims of superiority?

I had Kenneth help me remove all the material and burn it. I didn't want the household to be smeared by Algie's traitorous leanings.

Still in shock, I spent days wandering the house, more fresh and welcoming than the days before the fires. Who would grace those rooms now? Certainly not Prunilla's family, not sister Millicent and her questionable aristocrat husband. The thought sickened me. I was surprised they weren't banging at the door to be left in.

It turned out they did want to move in, but were advised by Freddie to wait until the reading of the will. Given the snail's pace of English legal procedures, this event did not occur for many weeks. The lawyer came to the estate because so many of us were named.

Prunilla's family arrived days early to go about and plan changes to the house. I booked them into the spidery Mustard and Gherkin suites and arranged a menu of the most archaic Cornwall cuisine. Her parents fought with Millicent over who would take over the refurbished family apartments. Letitia just rolled her eyes while observing their crass behavior.

The reading was long and suspenseful. The first surprise was a granting of the estate to a foundation, The Mystic Hues Theatre, in memory of Barnaby, Ravina, and Prunilla herself. Its purpose was to mount a drama festival during the summer season, provide housing for retired or disabled actors, and offer workshops in all the theatre arts and crafts.

That announcement sent the Crisp family into shouts and charges of a lawsuit. Calmed down, the lawyer outlined their monetary gifts. She granted her parents "sufficient funds to pay for their funerals and burials, since they certainly did not pay for mine." Although she left nothing to Millicent and her husband, she arranged small trusts for their children "who will need something at maturity because their parents will have spent it all." Her brother, of whom she never spoke, received £5,000 "for never siding with the rest of the family in their belittlements and doubts." It turned out he had moved to New Zealand when nineteen to raise kiwis.

Prunilla left a private letter for Letitia, and granted a portion of the estate lands be reserved in perpetuity for hunts. To the absent Mrs. Anvil she granted all the jewelry belonging to Ravina, and to Letitia all the remaining family jewelry.

Freddie was to head the Board of Directors of the new foundation until such time as an administrator was hired. It was hoped the Board would retain him as chief economic officer. Each staff member received monetary gifts much larger than that given the Crisps, as well as permanent tenure in their positions, which included retirement in the house, if they wished, along with a large pension. Prunilla understood the pride in their work and the value of continuing them on so the foundation could focus on its mission.

Great Aunt Nan was to return from Chilsworth to her honored place as Lady de Loverly. That was one cause for celebration later among the staff, who were pleased she could return to her old suite.

What about the yapper, Glocky? Willets took him to the kennels, where he turned out to be a she. Impregnated by a spaniel, the weird hybrids lost much of their terrier bad qualities and lived happily ever after while running loose. Letitia took in Algie's hounds, while the long-hidden Shires returned to entertain future guests with carriage rides.

As for me, Prunilla proved most knowing. I was to leave the estate and never return. She sweetened the command with a generous financial gift to help me off, and a private note.

Dearest Eddie Quirk,

My partner in crime. It is never too late to strike out anew and take chances in a strange land. There are libraries everywhere to satisfy. Your gift at cocktails will draw friends like a fish hooks a cat. I foresee terrible days for this island. It is no place for sensitive souls.

Go now, while you can. Perhaps you will find the woman of your dreams there. I hope so. You are a good man.

Yrs forever

Cesilly

At my farewell party, Letitia came by with mock tears. "So I'll never have my special evening? Well, it would have been very sinful. Anyway, I've found the most charming gardener on my estate. Reginald may have lost it, but I haven't." She described Prunilla's note as being full of graciousness and appreciation. I handed over the butler recipes for cordials and brandies to Kenneth, now promoted to major domo.

Freddie and I had a private last sit-to with brandy. "I'm changing my ways, Eddie. All this tragedy has pointed out the importance of a simpler life. I will no longer invest in German industries even though they produce a good return."

I told him about the Nazi cache from the secret room, and suggested he as good as supported that ugly movement. I spoke close to his face, virtually spitting in it.

"I deserve all your revulsion, Eddie. I was carried away by all the money coming in. Remember how I gained along with the estate. My greed has made me wealthy, but I must make amends. I'll contribute it to charities. As for my financial management, I'll stay within the Empire. Philip is pointing me to profitable Australian firms."

"Be honest, Freddie. You know if war strikes England, this is the time to invest in flight and munitions. Get in before others realize what is happening."

He then admitted patriotism wasn't his primary motive, that he remained lustful in several ways. We agreed friendship could thrive despite our differences, and promised to keep connected. I needed his smartly-worded letters to keep me on top of Slanderley life.

Epilogue

I departed about a month later, all my earthly goods in the hold of the Queen of the Sea. From New York I enjoyed the train cross country to Los Angeles. That city was attracting many from both Europe and England. Its endless sunny days and palm trees evoked an endless Eden, an escape from likely death, or in my case, a different life.

In no time I was friends with Hungarian and German refugees. Many had been writers, artists, composers, and actors affiliated with cinema in their home country, and found welcome in Hollywood. My first job in fact was replacing the vacationing butler for a popular Hungarian Jewish actor who changed his name for American movies. He suggested I might enjoy work as an extra and directed me where to go.

I was successful there, though I disliked the boredom of the job. Most fellow workers were Americans still climbing out of the Great Depression and happy to stand for hours in exchange for the week's food. One day I was called to play a businessman and sit at a desk. The director looked at me and gave me a line, "I agree." When he heard my English accent, he was not only delighted, he sent me over to Central Casting.

And so I achieved a small fame in the movies, where my British accent and experience brought me many character roles. You have perhaps seen me in more than one Fred Astaire movie where I play a butler. It seems Slanderley was preparing me for this all along, my ability to control my face and stature, and lie easily.

Thoughts of Slanderley disappeared from my mind until a few years later, when a book sketching some features of the events reported her rocked the best seller list. During Prunilla's hospitalization, her sister Millicent weaseled out stories about Slanderley. She contacted a well-known writer who was fascinated by the story and arranged a contract so each would benefit. Millicent need only jabber while the writer did all the work in exchange for the fame. She understood the need to cast the story as a modern fairy tale, complete with wicked queen Ravina, witch Mrs. Anvil, innocent and simpering victim Prunilla, and tortured lover Algernon. I seemed to take the form of a troll. In real life we were all less interesting, except to ourselves.

Now in the fall of my life, an era when unbarring the "real story" is in vogue, I feel released to expose the facts, unblemished. For those who wish a careful comparison of the two books and find inconsistency, I can only aver without hesitation that mine is the correct version, whatever the objections from the writer or her representatives. She may think me her creation, but were it not for my action and those of others, she would have no story. We have both lived well off of it.

And what of Mrs. Anvil?

That poor creature, burned in a house fire that killed her husband, given charity by the Elmsby family, provided they adopt her daughter as their own. Then she had to suffer as she watched that daughter at the hands of a psychopath, and sent into further mental persecution upon the discovery of murder. Out of the ashes arose a phoenix.

After Sloth pulled her from the fire, she faced months of painful rehabilitation. The doctors were much more skillful than the first time she suffered burns. They recreated the face that was the seed for Ravina's beauty. During my visits, she consoled me and counselled me. Long after I left the country she returned to Slanderley, preferring its solitude. Freddie called one day to say she had married Sloth, a most unimaginable, even ridiculous thought. He assured me they were most happy, having retired to the Canary Islands.

Freddie thrived as the director of Slanderley. Now that so many thespians appeared for workshops or rest and recuperation, he faced a steady stream of handsome men for entertainment. It was not long before he invited one to move into what were once the Lord and Lady's apartments. Ian's gentle sweetness compensated for Freddie's cynicism—or so he claimed in letters to me. He also became celebrated for his foresight regarding the munitions industry at home and joined several Boards of Directors. There his skills contributed to the war effort so well that he received Honors.

Freddie continued to speak with Philip on the phone. His wealth and fame grew. Running for the Australian Parliament, he fostered legislation in support of the arts, and was a benefactor to music conservatories and dramatic academies. He never married, though. Sadly, he died in 1941 when a he was gored by the runaway steer he was trying to capture. Half of his estate went to the schools and the other to his siblings and their children. Freddie said Philip never mentioned Ravina, yet certainly never forgot her.

My life changed in a most surprising manner. I was on the set for a new mystery film when my script directed me to order a maid, a walk-on, to straighten some pillows. During the rehearsal, I turned to speak to the maid and found myself face-to-face with Rose. We stared speechless until the director reminded us we had work to do. After he yelled, "That's a take," we approached one another warily.

"Lunch at the canteen?" I asked.

"A quick one. I'm due at my other job at two, and I'll need time to change before then."

Despite the crowd we managed to find seats in a corner where we wouldn't have to shout.

Following the usual prattle about the weather and Hollywood, we relaxed.

"I only arrived two months ago," noted Rose between sips of coffee. "I didn't know you were working here."

I told her about my unexpected luck, how cosmopolitan the industry had become with all the refugees and emigrants. I mentioned how Prunilla provided the funds to start over. "And what about you? After you left Nan I heard nothing from nor about you? I felt quite the idiot to let you go that way."

She frowned and sighed. "I daresay I was an idiot as well. I moved to a manor near Dover and met someone at the pub. He was an auto mechanic, very successful, more managed his shop than worked on the cars. He had--what's it called--charisma--a natural attraction that drew everyone toward him. I was surprised when he proposed. I became a housewife with my own cook and maid."

"Sounds wonderful. So why are you here?"

She stared down at the table. "He was very nice to me in every way. Given his popularity he belonged to many groups and was out several nights a week. One evening I went into his den, which he kept meticulously ordered, just mindless of where I was. I saw a paper under his desk and picked it up. It was in his handwriting, clearly notes for some kind of spying on behalf of the Germans. I was appalled. He was a master at disguise. I was just part of his proper front."

"So did you report him?" (And I thought I'd experienced drama.)

"Not immediately. I quietly prepared to leave without his suspecting. I was frightened to cross the Atlantic, ships threatened by U-boats. But I was even more afraid of my life were I to turn him in. His cronies would know and come for me."

"That must have been a terrifying time."

"I lied and said Nan was ill, that I wanted to see her at Slanderley. I packed a small bag, sewed money in my coat, and left from Liverpool. Funny, despite the U-boats I felt safe once the liner left port." She tapped her watch and before leaving agreed on a dinner date.

In time I learned how she worked for a dress designer's boutique, her experience as a lady's maid coming handy. Expats told her about temporary work on the sound stages and she signed up. Only by chance was she called in off an extras' list the day I was on set.

In time we moved beyond our past, namely my insensitivity toward her. Within a year she became my wife and moved into my Spanish Mission mansion in Pasadena. The California sunshine healed her spirit, with mine, and we proved that love born in adversity ages most fine.

Acknowledgements

I first composed what I called *Slanderley* in the mid-1970s. I had read *Rebecca*, Daphne du Maurier's best-selling novel. The husband's murder of his first wife struck me as essentially immoral, however his rationalization. The first line of that book is famous for its brilliance and recognizable in the first line of this one. It became a film as well, directed by Alfred Hitchcock. My apologies to the author, a writer who has gone out of favor but deserves reconsideration.

Conceiving of a different direction for the plot, I needed a fairly omniscient if clueless narrator. In the original novel, the second wife told the story. To my surprise Edmund Quirk, showed up uninvited to recount his experiences. As will be evident to those familiar with the novel, I have taken the key characters and added more of my own. They created the mysteries within, and at one point I was not sure who killed whom. Nor did I expect them to be so ridiculous at times, very unlike the original.

Some familiar with du Maurier will recognize hidden ties. Menabilly was the name of her house in Cornwall, and the model for Manderley. She loved the isolation, the privacy of the place. She was unhappy with reviews of *Rebecca* for their reference to the book as a mystery, when she intended it to be a study in jealousy. That theme runs through my parody as well in honor of her purpose.

My original draft was a novella. Passed among friends, it garnered praise, but I did not take it seriously. I was a serious college professor, not a fiction writer, let alone of humor. The manuscript sat for over forty years. After retirement I happened upon a new writing critique group. I decided to join because I was preparing a family history/memoir, *Gypsy and the Genius*. Having completed that manuscript, I did not want to leave the monthly exchange, so I submitted the first chapter of this story. The result was unanimous, that I must take it expand and continue to work on the novel.

This "Sunwrite Group" consisted of most astute and diverse writers, fiction and nonfiction. Much of the strength of the story is due to their specific advice and questions. Massive bouquets to Kathy Andrew, Marsha Trent, Susan Salenger, and Barbara Sapienza. Any errors are my own fault.

Also thanks to all my friends at The Sitting Room, A Community Library, who encourage my writing. When I retired, I said I had no intention to write another book, that it was too exhausting. I kept to that promise for ten years while people kept asking me what was next.

Other writers popped in to influence my words. During the final edit I was rereading much by and about Virginia Woolf and Bloomsbury. Sentences and phrases crept into the story, along with ideas for description or structure. My style is in no way Woolfian, yet I owe her a major debt for breaking up my usual patterns.

I sign off with sad memories to Rupert, who sat on my computer or interrupted me to be fed. Without his nagging I would never get away from the keyboard for a much needed break.

As always, my husband Michael Orton suffered through the worst periods, when I was about seeming to pay attention yet in "writing brain." When he said he liked the manuscript, I knew it was ready. Hence my dedication to him.

To My Readers

If you have enjoyed this book, or even if you didn't like it, please take a few minutes to write a review, whether on Powell, Goodreads, Kobo, Amazon, or your favorite book review spot. I value your feedback.

I support Independent Booksellers as much as possible. If you liked my book, let your local bookstore people know. They can order it through Ingram, the book distributor..

Claricestasz.com provides a way to contact me directly, and discusses my other books.

For my author updates, check Facebook:
www.facebook.com/ClariceStasz

I also keep a blog, *Charting Lives*, devoted to those who enjoy family history, writing memoirs, or nonfiction research:
Biographymemoir.net

Hope to meet some of you, digitally or otherwise!
Thank you.

About the Author

Clarice Stasz, Ph.D. is Professor Emerita of History from Sonoma State University. Prior to her over three decades at that school she was a Social Researcher at Johns Hopkins University.

Her trade books include *American Dreamers: Charmian and Jack London*, *The Vanderbilt Women*, and *The Rockefeller Women*, all published by St. Martin's Press. Her biography *Jack London's Women* is published by University of Massachusetts Press.

She is also author or co-author of six textbooks concerning gender roles, social simulation, and social control. She was a young professor just as the 1970s women's movement was underway, so she was particularly drawn to the condition of women in society and in history.

She has been a lifelong musician: piano, cello, percussion, flute, ukulele, and vocalist. She started the Uke Club in her town before the instrument became a rage. She is always in a band or a chorus.

Along the way a new muse appeared: songwriter. Her first performed song, Gassy Woman, has made her well-known within a very select group of San Francisco Bay Area musicians.

Her next book, *Gypsy and the Genius*, is a family history and partial memoir, due in late 2016. It addresses her Czech-Hungarian ancestors, their lives in Cleveland, and her own in New Jersey.

SLANDERLEY

CPSIA information can be obtained
at www.ICGtesting.com
Printed in the USA
FSOW03n0835200616
21717FS